OTHER BOOKS BY JAMES WILLIAM JONES

The Last Viking
Wilhelm's Thousand-Year Quest to Regain Valhalla
(ISBN 978-0-595-51095-5)

Triple CROSSED

JAMES WILLIAM JONES

iUniverse, Inc.
New York   Bloomington

Triple Crossed

iUniverse books may be ordered through booksellers or by contacting:

iUniverse
1663 Liberty Drive
Bloomington, IN 47403
www.iuniverse.com
1-800-Authors (1-800-288-4677)

Because of the dynamic nature of the Internet, any Web addresses or
links contained in this book may have changed since publication and
may no longer be valid. The views expressed in this work are solely those
of the author and do not necessarily reflect the views of the publisher,
and the publisher hereby disclaims any responsibility for them.

ISBN: 978-1-4502-5852-4 (pbk)
ISBN: 978-1-4502-5853-1 (ebk)

Printed in the United States of America

iUniverse rev. date: 10/8/2010

CHAPTER 1

Cardinal Peter A. Stancampiano sat in his office in the Vatican watching the clock on his desk. Almost six o'clock. He had been adamant about arriving before six. He drummed his manicured fingers on the desk. Finally, the phone rang.

"Yes, I am expecting Monsieur Chevalier," he said to the Swiss Guard. "Please show him in."

The cardinal walked to his office door and opened it just as Alix, the Swiss Guard, dressed in a simple solid blue version of the more colorful tri-color grand gala uniform and a black beret, appeared escorting a visitor. The visitor was equally tall and ramrod straight. He carried a large leather briefcase and wore an exquisitely cut black suit with a crisp, white shirt. Cardinal Stancampiano appreciated quality and his visitor exuded expensive yet subdued taste.

"Come in, Monsieur Chevalier. Thank you, Alix. That will be all. You may be excused. I will tell Fritz you have left when he arrives."

"I should stay until he arrives, your Eminence. It is strictly prohibited for me to leave my post until my replacement arrives."

"It is all right, my son. Monsieur Chevalier is here to protect me in case we are overrun with Huns," said Cardinal Stancampiano with a chuckle. "It has been many centuries since we have been attacked. I will give my word

1

to your captain if he asks. I think he will believe me. Don't you?"

"Yes. Of course, your Eminence. I will see you next week. I have the weekend off. I am taking a short holiday."

"Have a wonderful time."

When Alix left, Cardinal Stancampiano motioned toward his guest chair.

"Please have a seat, Monsieur. I assume you brought the money with you."

"Of course, your Eminence. I am a man of my word," said Monsieur Chevalier with more than a little sarcasm in his voice. He patted the briefcase at his side.

"That is a beautiful case," remarked Cardinal Stancampiano, rubbing his hands together in anticipation.

"I had it made especially for you, your Eminence. The leather is Moroccan."

Cardinal Stancampiano resisted the temptation to open the case immediately, saying, "If you will excuse me, I have a small detail to attend."

He opened the door and walked to the Swiss Guard station, turned the logbook around, and found the last entry. Cardinal Stancampiano took out his pen, signed out his visitor, and carefully entered the time as 17:59.

That was a short visit, he mused as he walked back toward his office.

He saw Fritz approaching and called to him.

"Good evening, Fritz. It is good to see you this evening. I have a large favor to ask of you. Would you please go to the cafeteria and bring me a cup of tea. Please ask Mina to brew it for me. She knows exactly how I like it.

Thank you. You are a good young man to put up with my idiosyncrasies."

"No problem, your Eminence. We are here to protect and to serve."

"That is not what they mean by service, but thank you. Why don't you get yourself a cup of coffee or tea? It is very quiet tonight. Put it on my charge."

"Thank you, your Eminence. I will be right back."

"Don't hurry, Fritz. I will be in my office working. I will probably be here late tonight."

When Cardinal Stancampiano returned to his office, he placed the brown leather briefcase on his desk and opened the clasps. The stacks of hundred dollar bills were neatly separated by handmade leather dividers, like an egg carton except the eggs were replaced by 10,000 crisp American bills bearing the likeness of Benjamin Franklin.

"How do I know these are real, not counterfeit?"

"How do I know your merchandise is real?" countered Monsieur Chevalier. "If we can't trust each other, who in this world can we trust?"

"When do I get the rest of my money?"

"I prefer to wire it to a Swiss account. I do not like the idea of carrying around this much money. Believe it or not, Cardinal, the world is full of dishonest people. Just remember, I do not want anyone to know about this transaction any more than you do. I will keep my end of the bargain, as well as the secrecy of our agreement, and I expect you to do the same. Agreed?"

"Agreed. Now follow me. We do not have much time. Fritz is conscientious. He will not leave his post very long."

Cardinal Stancampiano opened the door and cautiously peered down the hallway.

"Quick, follow me."

The two men were a study in contrast, one rather short and rotund wearing the cardinal red robes of the priesthood hurrying conspiratorially toward the staircase followed closely by a tall gentleman of military bearing in a tailored Italian suit. They quickly mounted the towering marble stairs to the next floor.

Stopping on the top landing, Cardinal Stancampiano whispered as he gasped for breath, "Wait here. I pass the door to the Pope's apartment on the way to the Swiss Guard station. I'll unlock the door and leave it ajar. When I distract the Swiss Guard, slip into the apartment. The Pope is away. No one enters his apartment except for the morning cleaning servants."

As the cardinal returned down the long hallway from the Swiss Guard station, he glanced back and saw the Swiss Guard was already engrossed in his magazine. He opened the door to the papal apartment and slipped inside. He swept the wall by the doorframe with his hand until he found the switch. The light revealed Monsieur Chevalier standing placidly in the middle of the room, hands in his pockets.

"Well, we made it this far, your Eminence. What do we do next?"

"I will do my part. The rest is up to you," said the cardinal walking briskly toward a large painting on the wall. He grasped one side of the frame and swung the priceless Raphael out from the wall, revealing a large safe. He immediately began opening the combination lock.

The safe opened with a solid clunk. Reaching inside,

Cardinal Stancampiano removed a large gold box, obviously heavy, covered with precious stones and elaborately engraved in Latin. He set the gilded box on a table and looked at Monsieur Chevalier.

"This is as far as I can go. The only key is worn by the Pope. He never removes it."

Monsieur Chevalier approached the box, obviously savoring the experience, looking at it with admiration.

"So this is where you keep them," he said without looking at the cardinal. "A sight few men have seen. I am humbled, your Eminence."

He took out a flat leather packet from his coat pocket and unzipped it. He examined the lock on the gold box and then his assortment of tools. Choosing one, he inserted it into the lock and, after a few deft motions, a click indicated the box was no longer locked.

"This lock is over a thousand years old, Cardinal Stancampiano. If I were you, I would suggest to his Holiness that he replace it lest it be compromised by some unscrupulous gent who would steal the most precious of treasures."

Cardinal Stancampiano ignored the remark and watched carefully as his visitor regarded the sacred box with reverence, obviously relishing the moment.

Monsieur Chevalier opened the lid carefully and examined the contents. He gently, reverently, removed part of the contents and then, just as carefully, replaced the rest and relocked the golden box.

"That amount will not be missed, I assure you, your Eminence. Now, let us retrace our steps and I will be out of your life forever."

"When will I get the rest of the money?"

"It will be in your new account tomorrow morning. I advise you to show restraint when you spend it, your Eminence. It would look unseemly for a man of God such as you to suddenly acquire accouterments unbecoming of your station."

"You needn't worry about me, Monsieur Chevalier. I have plans for the money and I will have a story to explain it."

"Since we shall not meet again, I will say goodbye here, your Eminence. Now if you will kindly distract the Swiss Guard, I will take my leave."

CHAPTER 2

Joe McPherson could hear a far-off ringing. The sound got closer and closer. *It must be time to get up. That damn alarm clock.*

Gradually Joe realized, *it couldn't be the alarm clock. I haven't set the alarm in years. I don't even have a fucking alarm clock. Why in hell won't that damn thing shut up?*

Joe rolled over in his bed and started patting the nightstand. He knocked off the empty two-liter plastic bottle that had formerly contained Popov vodka and heard it bounce away on the bare hardwood floor.

Must be the phone, he thought through the mist. *Why is the damn phone ringing?*

He finally felt the familiar shape of his cell phone. It was vibrating and ringing. He tried to focus on the lighted face of the phone. No name. Must be a wrong number. He pushed the green bar on his Treō to answer and immediately pushed the red bar, cutting off the call.

Two a.m. Got to be a wrong number. He slammed the phone down and mashed the pillow into a less uncomfortable lump under his head.

Seconds later the phone started ringing. Joe grappled for it again and this time barked, "You have a wrong number. Don't call me again."

Surprisingly, before he could hang up, he heard a response.

"Joe. Joseph McPherson? This is Cardinal, uh, Father O'Riley. I need to talk to you."

"Father O'Riley? Father O'Riley from the Diocese?" Joe slurred into the phone. "I can't talk. Call me tomorrow." Joe hung up the phone and passed out into a fitful sleep.

When the phone rang again it was well past at ten o'clock that morning. Joe McPherson was propped up on his pillow sipping a cup of instant coffee.

"Hello. Yes. How are you Father O'Riley? I'm sorry, I should call you Cardinal O'Riley. It must be almost eight o'clock in Rome."

Joe instinctively pulled up the sheet across his bare chest, and just as quickly mentally chided himself for being stupidly self-conscious.

"Joe, I need a favor," continued Cardinal O'Riley in his sonorous baritone.

"I don't know what…"

"Just hear me out, Joe. I need your help and I know you are no longer employed by the CIA. This is a very delicate matter, Joe, and you are in a position to provide a great service to the Church. Is there any reason you can't drop everything and come to Rome immediately?"

I don't have any commitments, if that is what you mean. However, I am, uh, low on funds just now."

"That is not a problem. I can help with that part."

"When do you want me there, Father, er, Cardinal?"

"You have reservations on the flight from Dulles to Rome tonight at 11:30. The airline is Lufthansa. You will pick up your ticket at the American Express office at the corner of 14th and K before five today. I have also arranged for a credit card and cash which they will have with the ticket. There will be a car at the airport in Rome to pick you up."

"Are you sure you want me to come, Cardinal? I have been going through..."

"I am sure. I will see you in Rome tomorrow. Try to sleep on the plane. You will have to hit the ground running here. And Joe, try to lay off the alcohol. I need you at full strength."

"I will be there, sir."

"Good. Now, you better get busy. I suspect you have things to do before you leave. Joe, you should plan to be gone for quite a while. This project may take weeks or even months. Are you prepared for that kind of commitment?"

"I will see you tomorrow. I will be ready to go to work on whatever you need. Thank you, sir."

"See you tomorrow," said Cardinal O'Riley hanging up the phone.

CHAPTER 3

Joe threw back the sheet and headed for the shower. His mind started to race through the things he needed to do before tonight. As the warm water cascaded over him, he thought about what he would need to take with him. His clothes were ragged. He hadn't bought a suit for years. Those last few years with the 'company' he had been relegated to the basement laboratory, just staying out of sight until his twenty years were up and they could pension him out. He was hung over most days and couldn't wait until he got home and mix a good strong martini.

They could have fired me, he reflected for the hundredth time. *At least they let me stay on until I could draw my pension. What if I can't do this thing? What if I let Cardinal O'Riley down? I can't let that happen.*

The sunlight was streaming through his bedroom window. *My God. I can't believe how dirty those windows are.* Joe walked toward his closet to look for something to wear. He kicked the vodka jug out of the way.

"Shit, I wish it was that easy to kick the habit," he said aloud.

He stared into the closet. He pulled the string twice before he remembered the bare light bulb had been burned out for weeks.

"Lucky it is daylight. Not much to see anyway."

With his foot, he stirred through the underwear and socks lying in a heap on the floor of the closet. He picked up a pair of semi-respectable socks and decided to forgo underwear altogether. *I need new stuff for this trip,* he rationalized.

In the corner of the closet was his black canvas carry-on. It was crushed under the weight of old shoes and clothing that had fallen off hangers.

"Need a new one anyway. I've had that thing since I got out of grad school," he said aloud to no one in particular.

Joe pulled on a black Jack Daniels tee shirt and a pair of faded jeans. He put on the rather stiff socks and slid his feet into the worn out Gucci loafers, probably the last remnant from the marriage. He tightened his belt and adjusted the extra material in the waistband so that the jeans didn't look so big.

When was the last time I ate? he thought. He took a look in the full length mirror on the closet door and decided he wasn't ready for GQ.

Joe passed the front desk on his way out.

"Jack, have my bill ready. I'm checking out of this place today."

"Bring cash or you don't take your clothes," Jack responded without looking up.

"They're all yours, Jack baby. Do with them as you will."

"Sure, Joe. Tell you what. I'll keep them for you. You'll be back."

"We'll see about that, Jack Baby. We will see."

The sun felt good as Joe turned north on 23rd Street and headed toward the Foggy Bottom metro station. He walked by the new row of sorority houses that faced the street. He had met Kim at a party in the old Kappa

Kappa Gamma house. *Those were the halcyon days,* he reminisced.

He was in graduate school at GWU and she was a senior majoring in political science. Molecular biology was just taking off and he was at the forefront of the technology. How lucky to be at the right place at the right time. Dr. Horowitz liked him the best. He always knew that.

I could have graduated a year earlier, he thought, *but I wanted to stay on and work with Bernard. We were that close to cloning. The Nobel was hanging out there for the taking. The days rushed by in a whirlwind. I lived well on the NSF grant. Every day I felt the adrenalin rush when I woke up. I had to make myself go to sleep. How I wish it could have lasted.*

Joe walked to the traffic circle and headed east on K Street. He remembered how smitten he was with Kim when they first met. He was just a small town boy from Iowa State on a fellowship at GWU getting a Ph.D. in molecular biology. The first member of the McPherson family to graduate from college, much less to get a Ph.D. Kimberly was the daughter of a United States senator. He had never met anyone that was in Congress, much less a senator. Senator Krauss. His mother almost fainted when he told her. 'Too bad your father is not alive to see this', she would say, over and over. The good memories came flooding back as he walked in the spring sunshine. It seemed like it was always spring back then.

The marriage had started out well enough. He wanted to take the post doc. Kim wanted to be settled and buy a house. Her friends were already having babies. The senator made sure Joe got the job at the CIA. Good ol' Senator Krauss. Joe never could figure out how he could live as he did on a senator's salary. The Krausses' did not come from money, but somehow they lived like it.

Joe liked the job with the 'company', but it was clear that he was never going to be able to provide for Kim in the way she was accustomed. The harder he worked, the further in debt they got. The house, the cars, the vacations with Kim's friends eventually overwhelmed the government pay scale. Joe turned to drinking and Kim turned to K Street. Apparently, money flows down K Street toward the Capitol Building and soon Kimberly was spending time with one of the lobbyist that frequented her father's office on The Hill. Two years of a disintegrating marriage was enough. They went to see Father O'Riley a couple of times for counseling, but Joe knew it was over. Funny, really, how Father O'Riley had been their counselor before they were married, and then again, when the marriage was ending.

Just like a priest, he mused. *They always get you coming and going.*

O'Riley was already a force in the Church, even back then. He would have never have met O'Riley except for the senator. It was obvious to everyone that O'Riley knew how to cultivate the rich and powerful to achieve his own personal ambitions

Joe turned the corner at 15th Street and walked into the American Express office. He briefly stood in the short line and was directed to an agent at a desk by the window.

"Hi. I'm Joseph McPherson. I think you have tickets for me," he said in his most professional voice to the well-groomed young woman.

Glancing up at him, she immediately noted his long, unkempt hair and shabby clothes.

"I will need two forms of identification, please.

Preferably your passport and drivers license," she spoke quickly in a monotone.

A dagger stabbed at Joe's heart. *My God, where is my passport? I hadn't even thought of that. I can't get out of the country without it.* Joe fumbled through his wallet. He pulled out his driver's license and his debit card. He had long since had his credit cards revoked.

"These will have to do for now. I left my passport at home," Joe lied.

His heart was still pounding from the shock of realizing he didn't know the whereabouts of his passport, much less, if it was still valid. The agent looked at the identification and glanced again at his clothes.

"I will have to get approval from my supervisor before I can release your card, money, and tickets. I will be right back."

Joe watched her walk to the back of the room and confer with an older woman. They looked up at Joe a couple of times and typed something into the computer. They looked at Joe again and then the agent returned to her desk.

"Here is your ticket for Rome," she explained as she placed the ticket envelop in front of Joe. This envelop contains $3,000 dollars. Please count it before you leave the desk. Here is an American Express Gold Card in the name of Dr. Joseph McPherson. You will have to activate it before you can use it. Would you like me to do that for you?"

"No. I think I can handle it myself. By the way, where will you be sending the monthly bills?"

"This is an American Express internal account, Dr. McPherson. The invoice will be handled by the cardholder.

You are the assignee. Now, if you will sign here indicating you have received these items, we will be finished."

Joe scribbled his illegible signature on the document, put everything into the manila envelope on the desk, and left. Once outside, he raced for the McPherson Square metro station. He stuffed one of the crisp new twenties into the ticket machine, selected the value, grabbed his fare card, and rushed down the escalator to the track to wait for a train. Only one stop to Foggy Bottom. Joe, exited the car, ran up the moving escalators, and headed down 23rd Street to his room.

Where did I put that damn passport? Joe racked his brain as he half walked - half jogged down the hill and through the door of the Allan Lee Hotel.

"Back already?" snapped Jack as Joe started up the stairs.

"Not for long," Joe retorted.

Once inside his room, Joe looked around, searching for a clue.

Where would I have put the damn thing? When was the last time I saw it? Think. Think. The last time? It must be when I left the CIA. I had to have had it with me. It's part of the clearing process.

Finally, Joe saw the expensive aluminum Halliburton briefcase under the desk. Another reminder of Kimberly. He grabbed it and snapped open the chrome clasps. It wouldn't open. The rolling numbers on the combination lock read 494. *What was the combination? Of course. It was 007.* His inside joke. He dialed the combination and the case opened. There were his papers, just as they had been left almost a year ago. Joe remembered his last day at work. They had taken him out for lunch. By the time they returned to the office he was too buzzed to remember anything about clearing through HR.

Joe sifted through the documents and found the passport. He opened it.

I still have over a year to go before it expires.

Relief flooded through his body. He should have known it would be good. The CIA was good at paperwork. Attention to detail was their specialty. Joe put everything into the briefcase and headed back downtown.

On the way out he snapped, "Jack, have my bill ready."

"Whatever you say, Dr. McPherson."

"Just have it ready, asshole," said Joe as the door to the hotel closed behind him.

Joe took the Blue Line back downtown, exiting at the Farragut West station. He walked up toward Connecticut Avenue, passing the Mayflower Hotel, and entered Brooks Brothers. He bought three white shirts. Brooks Brother's shirts were worth the money. They lasted forever and never needed ironing. The next stop was Filenes' Basement back down the street. Joe was still a graduate student at heart. He refused to pay full price for expensive clothes, especially when you could get good quality for cheap.

Joe went up to the men's department on the second floor and bought two sport coats and three pair of pants. He found a roll-on suitcase in the luggage department. He purchased underwear and socks, some good ties, two Polo shirts, and two pair of shoes. Joe paid with the new American Express card.

After paying, he went back into the fitting room, changed into a casual outfit, and dumped his jeans and socks in the trashcan on the way out of the store. Dragging the carry-on suitcase, now packed for the trip to Rome, he stopped into Louis' Barber Shop at 20th and K and got his first haircut of the year. The several-days growth of his dark beard looked quite stylish with the fresh haircut. Joe couldn't resist looking at his new persona as he walked by the store windows. His dark hair, now graying at the temples, and blue eyes were inherited from his father. His proclivity for drinking was probably a genetic gift also.

At least I didn't inherit his bad temper. One thing about not eating, it takes the pounds off, he thought as he looked at his thin profile. *I will grab a bite at the Columbia Plaza before I leave for the airport.*

Joe knew he was avoiding eating because, for him, eating meant drinking. It had been many years since he ate without having a beer or wine. If he started drinking, he soon escalated to hard liquor. By the time he got back in his room, his devils were confined to the back of his mind. Blind drunk meant out of sight, out of mind.

When he entered the Allan Lee Hotel, he went directly to the front counter and rang the bell loudly.

"Can I get some service here, Jack? Do you have the bill ready?"

The door to the office opened and Jack came out and stood behind the counter.

"Look at this," he exclaimed. "The new Dr. Joe! What happened, Joe, did you find a wad of dough on the sidewalk? Did a rich uncle die?"

"Just give me the bill, Jack."

"Hold on, Dr. McPherson. The real question is do you have the cash?"

"Try me, Jack."

Jack pushed the bill across the counter. Joe took out

his wallet and peeled off several hundred-dollar bills. Jack looked surprised, opened the cash drawer, and made change.

"You can have anything I leave, Jack. If you don't want it, give it to someone that can use it."

"Maybe I'll save it for you, Joe. You'll be back and broke, like as not."

"I won't be back, Jack. You can count on that."

"We'll see, Joe. We'll just wait and see."

CHAPTER 4

The flight attendant woke him about two hours from Rome. Breakfast looked good considering it was plane food. There was something that resembled an omelet, sausages, and pancakes with a container of syrup. Joe ate the pancakes first. His body craved the sugar in the syrup. Joe knew drinking vodka, or any other strong alcohol for that matter, stimulates insulin production. That speeds up the glucose metabolism and can actually result in low blood sugar. When he quit drinking, which was seldom and short lived, he craved sugar.

How strange, he thought, *to be a biologist and know exactly how you are killing yourself and then to keep on doing it.*

The plane landed at da Vinci International Airport just after sunup. Joe was stiff all over and his neck felt like he had been hanged and left for dead. He had slept for most of the flight and the caffeine from the strong European coffee was beginning to provide brain stimulation. Joe took his carry-on bag from the overhead compartment and shuffled toward the mid-plane exit. The long ramp up to the glassed-in lobby was full of plodding, sleepy travelers. Signs led to the customs stations and after a perfunctory check of his passport and a stamp on his disembarkation card, he walked out of the receiving area.

He was greeted by scores of waiting family members and men in cheap suits holding placards with names printed with a magic marker. Near the end of the roped-off area, he spotted a cardboard placard with the machine printed name 'Dr. McPherson'. He motioned to the man holding it who immediately ducked under the rope and wrenched the handle of the suitcase from Joe.

"Follow me, sir. The car is just outside," said the man in heavily accented English.

Joe had to hustle to keep pace with his greeter. As soon as they passed through the automatic doors, Joe noticed a black Lincoln with dark glass everywhere except the front windshield. The back door was opened for him and he slid into the leather interior. He heard the trunk motor grind closed and the man got in behind the driver, leaned forward, and said something in Italian Joe couldn't catch. The car sped away into traffic, horn honking, swerving from lane to lane. Joe groped for his seatbelt, failed to find one, gave up, and held on to the door handle for dear life.

The limousine wove expertly through the turbulent Rome traffic. As they came in sight of the Vatican, the greeter opened his cell phone and pushed a speed dial button. He mumbled a few words. The car proceeded to the back of the Vatican and turned down an alley. The driver reached up and pushed a button on the rear view mirror that opened a garage door in the long stone wall. The Lincoln passed through the opening and the door closed securely behind. The car continued for several hundred yards inside the dimly lit corridor and stopped at a staircase with polished brass handrails. The greeter jumped out, came around to Joe's door, and opened it for him, indicating he should proceed up the stone staircase. When Joe reached the landing, a carved wooden door opened and Cardinal O'Riley offered his hand. As Joe grasped it, the cardinal pulled him into an embrace.

"Thank you for coming Joseph. Please come with me. Your luggage will be brought up later."

Cardinal O'Riley walked briskly down the carpeted hallway and entered a waiting elevator. As they rode up, Cardinal O'Riley began to explain.

"We are assembled in the second floor conference room, Joseph. We have been tracking your flight," said Cardinal O'Riley looking into Joe's eyes. "What we are about to tell you must not leave the room. You are not to discuss it with anyone except me. Five cardinals have been chosen to deal with this situation. I have been appointed to be in charge of the investigation."

"What kind of investigation? Are you sure I am the right person for this? I have never been an operative. I spent my years working on technology, not in the field."

"When you hear the problem, Joe, I think you will understand why I called you. I want you to realize the gravity of this problem. The Holy Father himself has chosen us for this assignment. He has appointed me to head the investigation. Joe, you may not realize, but I could very well become the next Pope. Think about it, Joe, the first Pope from the United States. The first Irish Catholic Pope. To be given this assignment validates my suspicions I could be in line for succession. We must not fail the Holy Father, Joe. Failure is not an option."

The elevator door opened and Cardinal O'Riley darted out of the elevator with Joe trailing along the richly carpeted hallway. Priceless artwork adorned the walls. They did not have to walk far until Cardinal O'Riley stopped at a door and grasped the handle, waiting for Joe to catch up. He swung open the door just as Joe approached and whisked him inside. Cardinal O'Riley entered in a flourish, his robes swirling around him.

When Joe entered the large conference room, he saw four men dressed in cardinal's robes sitting at a long oval table. Behind them was a glass wall of windows overlooking St. Peter's Square. The cardinals rose to greet him, extending their hands, and saying their names, each with a different accent. The conclave consisted of the Church's holiest men. Joe, overwhelmed by the attention and the circumstances, immediately forgot the names as soon as they were spoken.

"Would you care for a cup of cappuccino?" asked the short, swarthy gentleman who seemed to have a Spanish accent. "Cappuccino was invented by the Capuchin friars several hundred years ago. We drink it here to remember them and, of course, because we like it also," he said with a wry grin.

"I think a cup would help tremendously," responded Joe. "Sitting up is not my favorite sleeping position."

"Good. This gives me an excuse to have another cup myself." He rose and glided to the counter and began to busy himself with the large silver machine. "Please get started. I can listen and make coffee at the same time."

Cardinal O'Riley, who was seated at the head of the table, began to talk. His voice was no longer conversational as it had been in the elevator, but took on the gravity of one presenting to an audience. Joe sensed O'Riley was assuming the role of authority.

"First of all," began Cardinal O'Riley looking at Joe, "I want to thank you for coming on such short notice and with so little explanation. You have already demonstrated your faith and commitment to the Church, but I assure you, this is only the beginning. What we are about to tell you concerns the most well guarded secrets of the Church. This matter involves the very foundations of our belief. What you learn here must not be discussed with anyone except for the men in this room and only then when absolutely necessary."

The other cardinals nodded in solemn agreement. A cup of cappuccino was placed in front of Joe and he sipped it without taking his eyes off Cardinal O'Riley.

Cardinal O'Riley continued, "Two days ago one of our own died. He was an old man, over ninety, and he had been elevated to cardinal many years ago. His name was Cardinal Stancampiano. He had been, so we all thought, a loyal and true man, the intimate of the last five Holy Fathers. He was a man we all turned to for advice and counsel. On his deathbed, when he was receiving last rights, he made a startling confession. He admitted he had sold a portion of our most holy of all relics to a stranger. He died almost immediately after his confession. It was as if his need to confess this egregious sin was the last thing that was holding him on this earthly plane."

Joe's mind raced ahead. *What was Cardinal O'Riley talking about? What could be that important to the Church?*

"Before I proceed, Joe, I need to provide you with the background you will need to truly appreciate the importance of these particular objects. I know you were raised in the Catholic Church, so I will not have to go into great detail. You know the story of the crucifixions of Christ. I will take up the story when Jesus in on the cross, having suffered and died. Jesus was a Jewish rabbi, as you will remember," continued the cardinal. "It is a practice of the Jewish faith, known as the Mosaic Law that a person hanged until death on a cross in the manner of our Lord must not be allowed to remain there at night, but should be buried before sundown. Joseph of Arimathea, a disciple of Christ, asked Pontius Pilate for the body of Jesus. Pilate was skeptical Jesus was actually dead, since many men who were crucified in this same manner lived throughout the night. Before dispatching the body to Joseph, he summoned a centurion to confirm the validity of their claims. The Roman centurion, just to make sure He was dead, used his long spear to puncture the side of Jesus. Jesus bled, but otherwise had no reaction, since He was, in fact, dead. Jesus was removed from the cross by His followers and taken to a tomb that had been prepared for a relatively wealthy merchant who was also a follower."

"I remember the story very well, Cardinal," said Joe.

"Good. It gets more interesting," responded Cardinal O'Riley. "Saint John recorded that Joseph was assisted in the burial process by Nicodemus, who brought a mixture of myrrh and aloes and included these spices in the burial cloth as per Jewish customs. We believe this preparation consisted of several ritualistic practices. First, the body was cleaned and the arms and legs were placed into a final resting position, legs together and arms folded across His chest. He would have been tied into this position by strips of linen. The body was groomed, similar to how we currently prepare a body for a funeral. It was at this time we believe the hair and beard of Jesus were trimmed and groomed. He was made to appear more like the holy rabbi that He was."

Cardinal O'Riley watched Joe's reaction in silence for a minute and then continued, "Mary Magdalene, who had accompanied Jesus on His journey to Jerusalem and witnessed His crucifixion, returned to the tomb the next morning with several other women. They had brought spices to anoint His body, as was the custom. She found the tomb empty. Later, Jesus appeared to her when she was alone. She did not recognize Him at first. This event has always perplexed scholars of the Bible, since Mary Magdalene was probably the closest person to Jesus of all of His followers. When she saw it truly was Jesus, she called Him Rabbi."

"And you believe she called Him Rabbi because He now looked like a Jewish rabbi?" added Joe.

"From the amount of hair that was removed," continued Cardinal O'Riley, "Jesus would have looked very different. Something that is not recorded in the Holy Scriptures, Joe, is that Joseph of Arimathea kept the hair and beard he trimmed from Jesus, as well as the bloody cloth He had been wearing at the time of His crucifixion. It is not uncommon to keep locks of hair from a departed loved one and certainly, Jesus was loved by His disciples. Joseph kept those relics of our Lord hidden away in a safe place. The Romans were trying to destroy Christianity and they believed that once Jesus was crucified, His followers would soon scatter. Of course, this did not happen. The subsequent resurrection of Jesus changed the course of history."

"Joe, now I must tell you something only a relative handful of men have known. The relics of Jesus, His hair and the cloth He wore on the cross, are here in the Vatican. They have been preserved for over two thousand years by the Church. They are the only proven sacred artifacts of Jesus. There are other relics that are claimed to be authentic, such as the loincloth at Aachen, Germany, but we have indisputable proof our relics actually belonged to Jesus. We have guarded them all of these years. In order to protect them, we kept them a secret. The more people that know the existence of something valuable, the more likely it is to be stolen."

"So why are you telling me this, Cardinal O'Riley? I can't think of any reason I need to know the inner secrets of the Church."

"You will. First, let me tell you only twelve people are allowed to know the secret at any time. All of them, until now, hold or held the rank of cardinal, and only those cardinals who are thought to be in line of secession to Pope are informed of the existence of the relics. Cardinal Stancampiano, who died three days ago, was the oldest of the twelve. Twelve is a special number in the Church and, throughout our history; we made sure these men are never in one place together. Someone must be alive to pass along the secrets of the Church. We make an exception when there is a conclave to choose a new Pope. Then we place our trust in the Lord to keep us safe."

Joe was beginning to feel uneasy.

"May I have another cup of cappuccino, please?" he asked.

Cardinal Sanchez of Spain smiled. He was amused at being asked to serve this stranger who held no rank in the Church, but he was a humble man and moved toward the cappuccino machine.

"In his last confession," continued Cardinal O'Riley, "Cardinal Stancampiano revealed he had sold part of the sacred relics of Jesus to a stranger."

Cardinal O'Riley paused for emphasis, and then he continued.

"The sale of relics is strictly forbidden by the Church. The Code of Canon Law states in Section 1190, it is absolutely forbidden to sell sacred relics. Cardinal Stancampiano has sinned grievously."

"When did this happen?" asked Joe.

"Unfortunately, we do not have an exact time. Cardinal Stancampiano had suffered a stroke and his speech was slurred. Further, he had endured a mild form of Alzheimer's for some years so his mental faculties were not that good before the stroke. What we do know is he said it had been many years ago. When pressed for a more definitive time, he said ten or fifteen, maybe longer. As I told you, he died soon after receiving last rites."

"So, now you think someone has hair and possibly blood samples of Jesus Christ?" said Joe as he sat back in his chair. "That explains why you called me. You need to know if it is possible to use them to create a clone of Jesus. Correct?"

"I'm afraid it is more complicated than that, Joe," continued Cardinal O'Riley. "We need someone to find out who took them and get them back."

Cardinal Sanchez pushed a new cup of cappuccino toward Joe. He spoke in accented English.

"We cannot tell the Swiss Guards, now can we? Do you think they could keep our secret? We cannot tell the Italian police. Their organization is very corrupt. The Americans? Everything leaks out of Washington. Even the bad habits of your president and the identity of your CIA operatives are disclosed."

Cardinal O'Riley continued, "You can understand

what would happen if this information was leaked to the public. If anyone knew we had the actual hair and blood of Jesus Christ, there would be a complete media panic. The science community would want to use this to sequence the genetic code and to determine if Jesus was an 'ordinary' man or if they could find something in his genetic makeup that would prove him to be supernatural. You will remember Jesus was born of a virgin. That fact raises some very interesting questions. The controversy could completely disrupt the work of the Church. Even the fact that the very existence of the relics was kept a secret for all these years would be highly controversial. Joe, we need you to find this material and get it back if possible. We are counting on you."

Joe leaned forward, cupped his hands around his drink and thought, *First, I just quit drinking and I'm having withdrawal. I have jet lag that feels like it could be terminal and now they want me to take on this impossible mission to find something that may have been stolen twenty years ago. At least I'm wide awake now.*

Joe stood up and walked to the window still holding his cappuccino in both hands. He looked out onto the plaza below him and saw the line of visitors that stretched for blocks waiting to enter the Basilica.

"Let's go through the possibilities," he said at last. "I am going to assume everything you have told me is completely true. First, it is odd an outsider would know about the existence of the relics. I will call them relics if you don't mind. I am having a hard enough time coping with just being here, much less having to find the actual remains of Jesus Christ. My first thought is another one of the twelve men who knew of their existence must be involved.

However, assuming Cardinal Stancampiano would never have sold to one of these men nor would they have had reason to buy from him would seem to eliminate everyone who knew of the existence of the relics. Clearly, that is not the answer. We must conclude others knew of the existence of the relics. Someone who had money."

"Next, we have to try to think about motive. Why would someone want part of these relics? Could it be a collector, seeking to acquire the ultimate in unique collectables? Who would believe you? How could you establish provenance? Not a likely motive."

"Let's assume this person had a desire to clone or reproduce Jesus Christ. For now, let's forget about a motive for wanting to do it, but concentrate on what they could do with these bits of Jesus Christ. Fifteen or twenty years is a long time in genetics. The field is changing so quickly the capability that existed at the time they were stolen is primitive compared to what we can do today. However, the person who obtained them may have realized the potential and wanted to obtain the samples before their true value would have been apparent to the cardinal."

"I am following you so far," said Cardinal O'Riley. "I agree with your logic. Now, where does that lead us?"

Joe began to pace slowly back and forth in the front of the room as he talked.

"First, we will assume the thief wants to clone Jesus," continued Joe. "He could, potentially, create an exact replica of him. Multiple clones would have the same exact appearance, except of course, for any differences that resulted from sickness or accidents occurred during pregnancy, childbirth, or childhood, etc. We don't really know what effect environment would have on human clones since, to our knowledge, none have been produced. We also do not know if a clone would think like the original since the brain is essentially blank at birth and we learn most of the things we know. However, if the clone did have supernatural powers, such as the ability to perform miracles, that would open up a whole new set of possibilities."

Joe stopped and looked out the window, lost in thought, then continued, "Secondly, let's assume the thief is more creative. There are genetic engineering techniques that can be used to modify humans born in the normal way. Somatic genetic engineering involves adding genes to cells other than egg or sperm cells. For example, if a person had a disease caused by a defective gene, a healthy gene could be added to the affected cells to treat the disorder. If this person or organization could isolate what I will refer to as the 'Jesus Christ' genes, then it may be possible to add these genes to a living human to duplicate his ability to perform miracles or return from the dead. I can certainly imagine this as being a great advantage in wartime. Also, it would be quite marketable to older humans who can afford to pay for another chance at life. The distinguishing characteristic of somatic engineering is that it is non-inheritable, i.e., the new gene would not be passed to the recipient's offspring."

Joe walked to the serving counter and set down his empty cup.

"Would you care for more coffee?" asked Cardinal Sanchez.

"No, thank you. I have imposed on you enough already." Joe continued, "Finally, we need to consider germline engineering. This process involves changing genes in eggs, sperm, or very early embryos. This type of engineering is inheritable, meaning the modified genes would appear not only in any children that resulted from the procedure, but also in all succeeding generations. Germline engineering would allow this person, or more likely a team of people, to implant specific genes into offspring that would still have most of the characteristics of their parents. The engineered offspring would still appear to be normal children, but would have these 'Jesus genes'."

Cardinal O'Riley stood and walked toward Joe. Putting his arm around him, the cardinal said, "I can see already we have chosen the right man that can help us solve this dilemma. Joe, you will take on this mission, won't you?"

"Cardinal, you may or may not have chosen the right person. That remains to be seen. However, you have chosen the available person. Since I now know the secret of the sacred relics, which is limited by canonical law to twelve men, I have to take the job. You can't tell anyone else unless you kill me."

It took a short while for the others to realize Joe was joking and finally there was muted laughter in the room.

"What do we do next, Joe?" said Cardinal O'Riley.

"I was just thinking about that. This is definitely a cold case. All we have to go on is the confession of an old man who had a stroke and possibly dementia. I think there may be a possibility it never happened at all. I assume there has been no contact with anyone demanding ransom for these relics. True?"

The cardinals nodded in agreement.

"There has been no report of anyone attempting to sell the relics, correct?"

"Correct," injected Cardinal Sanchez.

"For the time being, we must assume a theft has occurred. I will attempt to determine if and when it occurred, and of course, who is the thief? May I assume Cardinal Stancampiano lived here in the Vatican?"

"He has a small apartment on the ground floor. He was too frail to climb stairs."

"I would like to live in his apartment if it is permissible."

Nodding heads assured Joe.

"Please, don't change anything but the sheets. Who is his next of kin?"

"Cardinal Stancampiano outlived his siblings. He has not had family, to our knowledge, for a number of years. He will be buried by the Church and we will morn him," answered Cardinal O'Riley in his best clerical voice.

"You can often learn a lot about a person by looking through their possessions. I will use his office as well. Please, do not disturb his office. If you need to take any church materials or files, let me look through them before they are removed."

"Cardinal Stancampiano has not had any new projects for several years, Dr. McPherson. He was just living out his final days here at the Vatican. We could not bring ourselves to take him to a home for the elderly," said Cardinal Sanchez

"Excellent," exclaimed Cardinal O'Riley. "You can move in tonight. I will have your bag brought up by the driver. What are you going to do first, Joe? How do you intend to get started solving this conundrum?"

"First, I intend to take a long, hot shower. Second, I intend to try out Cardinal Stancampiano's bed and sleep for as long as possible. I will see you later today or possibly tonight. I would like very much to examine the remaining relics. I need to know exactly what we are dealing with here."

Cardinal O'Riley responded, "The Pope himself carries the only key. He wears the key on a gold chain around his neck that he never removes. We will have to determine a time to meet the Holy Father in his apartment. It might take a day of two to arrange. It is difficult to get onto the Pope's schedule. Is that everything?"

"It's everything I can think of for now. Good morning, gentlemen. It has definitely been an interesting couple of days."

CHAPTER 5

Joe woke slowly and his brain started to function. He looked around the small apartment, confused at first until he remembered he was in the Vatican, in Cardinal Stancampiano's bed.

What a difference a day makes, he thought. *What have I gotten myself into?* He fumbled with the nightstand light switch until it clicked and looked at his watch.

"Eleven thirty-seven. A.m. or p.m.? No windows," he muttered under his breath.

He had to go to the bathroom. As he swung out of bed, he felt slippers on the floor. Not his. Joe went to the bathroom and stayed to brush his teeth and splash water on his face. He returned and sat on the edge of the bed. He picked up a slipper. Red. Made by Prada. *Size 41. Forty-one,* thought Joe. *It can't be inches, not even centimeters. I have no idea how the Europeans measure shoe sizes. I'd guess this is about a size seven or eight in the U.S. The cardinal definitely had a small foot.* Joe had read that Prada now made the slippers for the Pope. He wondered if all the cardinals got them free. Prada was not cheap.

Joe walked to the door and found the light switches. The apartment was well furnished. The smell of an old man hung in the air, but the furniture was well made and in excellent condition. Some pieces appeared to be antiques, possibly very old. Joe knew very little about antique furniture, just a few visits to museums. Kim could probably estimate the price of everything in the room within a few percent. Kim was the ultimate consumer and connoisseur of expensive merchandise. She could take one look at someone and estimate the cost of everything they wore.

This looks like very expensive taste for a humble man of God. I wonder if this is typical of cardinals or if Stancampiano lived beyond his means? I will ask O'Riley.

Joe opened the closet. The red robes of the cardinal stood out immediately. As Joe slid the hangers along the rack, he noticed a row of suits. The labels read Henry Poole & Co., Gieves & Hawkes, Davies and Son, all from Savile Row. Probably handmade. Shoes were stacked neatly in their original boxes. Prada, Ferragamo, Berliti, A. Testoni, Crockett and Jones, and other labels Joe did not recognize.

Joe thought about his closet. *I sure hope someone is not going through my stuff and judging me by my clothes. They would probably be right, though.*

Joe opened what looked to be an antique armoire. He pulled out a large drawer and found a jewelry box containing gold chains, bracelets, rings, and cuff links. There was an entire box that contained gold crucifixes and rosary beads. The cardinal apparently liked gold.

This man was definitely a neat freak, he thought.

Everything was in the original box and the boxes were precisely arranged. Joe noticed a large walnut box. He carefully removed it and set it on the dresser. When he opened the lid, he was surprised to find almost a dozen watches, each mounted on a slowly rotating arm.

This must keep them wound, he surmised.

There were diamond studded Rolex's, Patek Philippe,

Girard-Perreguax, a Cartier Pasha, and a few brands that were unknown to him. Some appeared to be new. Others were clearly antiques.

Quite a collection, he contemplated. *This man liked to live well. Interesting. He could wear most of this stuff under his robes and no one else would even know he owns them. Purely ego? Is this cardinal hedonism?*

Joe walked to the bookcases that surrounded the cardinal's desk. *You can tell a lot by the books a man collects,* he thought. *You may read many books in your life, but the ones you choose to keep usually provide insight into your personality. Someone once said a writer is always autobiographical except for what they plagiarize. The books you choose to keep are likewise revealing.*

Cardinal Stancampiano had a rather eclectic taste in books. His college books, all in Italian, were neatly arranged by year of education through a Ph.D. in theology. *A very learned man,* thought Joe.

There were books on religion, comparative religion, philosophy, history, and many books on the history of the Church. There were learned tomes on men of various religions. There were books on the life of Buddha, Mohammad, and other religious figures through the ages. *Apparently, Cardinal Stancampiano studied his competition,* he thought. *I wish I could read Italian. I could spend a month or two here just reading.*

Joe noticed the books were dusty. They had not been read lately, probably for years.

Joe walked to the right side of the desk and pulled out a book from the case. It was an ancient book on the martyrs of the Church. This was an original, hand copied, and illustrated. He noticed several other books were of similar age and quality. There was no dust on these books; they had been handled recently. Joe carefully opened another one of the rare books and turned the pages. The gilded illustrations were beautiful and it was obvious the lettering was gold leaf.

Another little treat for our cardinal, thought Joe. *He certainly had a passion for the better things in life. I wonder where you buy something like this? This is definitely museum quality and probably came from one. I wonder if they knowingly sold it or if this was a midnight acquisition? Yes, you can learn a lot about a man by what he puts on his bookshelves.*

Joe spent the next hour mentally cataloging books and possessions. He had no idea of the value of the contents of the room because he had no reference points for the antique pieces nor the high-end clothing, watches, or jewelry.

How long had the cardinal owned them? How would one locate a market for collectors and connoisseurs for these items?

It was way above the pay grade of a government employee; that was for sure.

Joe glanced at his watch again and realized he still didn't know whether it was day or night. Finally, he thought of his Treō. The phone wouldn't work here in Italy, but the world clock should still be correct. Joe picked it up and found the time in Rome. It was 12:45 a.m.

Maybe I will go back to bed for a while, he thought. The next time he looked, it was 8:00 o'clock in the morning and he was ravenous.

CHAPTER 6

Tel Aviv, Israel

Myra Cohen waited outside the offices of Meir Snir. She was somewhat apprehensive, but confident. She had been racking her brain for hours, since she had gotten a call from Meir's secretary, to come in for the meeting. She knew she hadn't done anything that would rise to the level of either a stern lecture or kudos from the director. It had to be one or the other. It always was either something bad or something good. No in-between. The director didn't waste time on trivial matters.

Finally, the door opened and a man appeared, backing out of the office while shaking hands with the director.

"Yes sir, Mr. Director. I will handle it personally. I can assure you the matter will be disposed of immediately," he managed to say without taking a breath.

"Very good, Jake, I will look forward to your report in the next day or so. Have a nice weekend," said the director, knowing Jake would have a crappy weekend.

Director Snir looked around the waiting room and spotted Myra.

"Come in Myra. It has been quite a while since we have had the opportunity to chat."

The director turned and disappeared into his office before Myra could cross the room at her usual high-octane pace. When she entered the room, he indicated a chair in front of his desk and pulled out a thick file from his center drawer. Myra knew he kept the hot cases in the center drawer. The director opened the file as she sat down and read silently for about a minute. Finally, he pushed his glasses up on his large, ruddy, vascular nose and cleared his throat.

"I have a rather strange one for you, Myra. This is one of those instances where the facts don't make much sense, but it has a smell. I can smell a problem coming before it gets here. I definitely think this one has a strange odor."

"What can you tell me about the case, Director Snir?"

"Myra, please call me Meir. You and I go back a long way. I remember the day you were born. Your father and I were as close as brothers. It is a shame he didn't live to see how you turned out. He died a hero's death and yet we cannot give him the credit he deserves. When you work for the Mossad, you get the dirty work and if you're really good, nobody knows you exist."

"Thank you, Meir. There is not a day that goes by I do not think about him."

"How is your mother? And your son?"

"My son is almost twelve now. Mother takes care of him for me."

"Well, I'm afraid she will have to do double duty for a few weeks, Myra. I am sending you to Rome and I don't know how long this assignment will last."

Meir Snir pushed the folder across the desk. Myra picked it up and began reading the file. As she read, the director began.

"This is an unusual one all right. It seems the Pope has brought in a former CIA man to live in the Vatican.

My informant tells me that there is a very high-level task force, consisting of five cardinals, the Pope himself, and this CIA man. Never have I ever seen anything like this happen, even at the penultimate old boys club. We need to check it out."

"But Director, what does this have to do with Israeli security? What do we care if the Pope has a CIA man on his staff? I don't see…"

"Myra, I told you the facts do not support my suspicions. However, one of the perks of this job is that I get to make the decisions, all the decisions. If I think it smells, then you have to find the stink. Those are the rules. Anyway, I have a few more tidbits to share with you. This new gentleman that now works for the Pope was discharged from the CIA because he is a lush. He hasn't been sober for years. Another thing that is interesting is that he is a biologist and he never spent any time in the field. He is a research weenie. Now, why would the Pope bring in an alcoholic, research nerd and team him up with five cardinals, one of whom will probably be the next Pope? Does that make any sense to you?"

"Actually, Director, nothing about the Catholic Church makes much sense to me. But, I can see this is unusual. However, I still don't understand what it has to do with us?"

"You know what, Myra? Neither do I. That is the reason you are going to Rome and find out for me. Take that folder with you. Your plane leaves tomorrow morning. Good luck and keep me informed. It was good seeing you again."

Myra walked out of the office and immediately began to think about how she was going to offload her current cases, say goodbye to her mother and Adam, and make the plane tomorrow. Another weekend spoiled. Sometimes she felt like quitting this goddamn job and this was definitely one of those times.

CHAPTER 7

A good hot shower had erased most of the remaining jet lag and Joe felt better than he had in years. *Nothing to drink for three days,* he thought. *I can't remember that happening for a long time. I'm hungry. I wonder where you eat around this place. I really don't crave a drink. It must be the excitement or something. I hope it doesn't come back.*

By the time Joe left the apartment, it was almost noon. He locked the door and headed for the Swiss Guard station to get directions to Cardinal O'Riley's office.

"Do you speak English?" Joe asked the Swiss Guard.

"I try, sir. May I be of assistance?" he replied with just a hint of an accent.

"Where can I get something to eat?" Joe asked rather sheepishly. It intimidated him that everyone seemed to speak several languages and his two years of college French had completely withered from lack of use.

"The cafeteria is about a ten minute walk from here, sir. You are a guest here at the Vatican. Just sign for your food. Your name will be in the computer." The Swiss Guard provided detailed directions to the cafeteria.

The Vatican proved to be a labyrinth of hallways and corridors. Joe finally found the cafeteria, took a tray from the stack, and pushed it along the metal rails as he picked items from the glass-covered display.

They seem to eat well here, he thought. The array of food was vast and well presented. His tray was full before he reached the main courses. As he headed for the cashier, he noted a well-stocked cooler of wines. There were wines from all over the world. Small, airplane size to half bottles and even a rack filled with full bottles. He wanted to reach for an interesting looking Merlot, but thought the better of it. *I know I won't stop at one. I better go with coffee today.*

He gave his name to the cashier and her nod indicated he was indeed in the computer. Joe was almost finished eating when Cardinal O'Riley appeared from behind.

"Hi Joe. I went by your room to see you and the Swiss Guard told me you were here. How do you like the food?"

"It's wonderful, Cardinal. I think I will gain weight if I stay here very long."

"It is good. However, like every cafeteria, it will become tedious eventually. No matter how hard they try, everything starts tasting the same after eating here long enough. I wanted to tell you we have an appointment with the Pope tomorrow at noon. His Holiness has decided to take his lunch in his apartments to make time to talk to you and show you the relics."

"That is wonderful, your Eminence. I never thought I would have the honor to meet him. You will have to educate me on how I should address him and how I should act in his presence."

"You will be fine, Joe. His Holiness is the most humble man I ever met. He is counting on you to help us. In the meantime, what do you need from me?"

"I have spent several hours going through the apartment. Did you know Cardinal Stancampiano has hundreds of thousands of dollars worth of personal belongings? He has gold jewelry, expensive watches, incredibly expensive suits, and priceless antique books. This is just what I have found so far."

"Father Stancampiano apparently had a rich patron. We all knew he had someone who was extremely generous. It is not uncommon to have a wealthy benefactor. They believe the prayers of someone like the cardinal can bring good fortune and health. I get presents from time to time from my old parishioners. The pay in this line of work is meager at best. I, of course, donate most of these gifts to the various charities I support."

"Of course, Cardinal. However, it seems Cardinal Stancampiano decided to use these gifts personally."

"It is of little matter, Joe. They are the property of the Church now that he is dead. They will be put to a good cause. I have to go now. Do you have keys to Cardinal Stancampiano's office?"

"Yes, I think so. I found a set of keys in his desk last night and the locks in the building are all the same brand. I tried the keys and his room key is on the set, so I think the office key will be there also."

"If you need help, the Swiss Guard will let you in. He has been instructed to give you whatever you need in your investigation. If you need to go anywhere in the city, call my secretary. He will arrange for transportation."

"Thank you, your Eminence. I think I am making some progress. I don't have much to go on yet, but I think I will make more progress once I get into his office."

"Very good, Joe. I knew I could count on you. Please call me Patrick or Pat. Patrick is my Christian name and I miss the informality of knowing people on a first name basis. If we are going to be working together on solving this puzzle, I want you to think of me as a co-worker and colleague."

"It will get little getting used to, Patrick. Now, I will get back to work."

CHAPTER 8

Joe spent the rest of the day in Cardinal Stancampiano's office. The keys did indeed fit the door and the file cabinets inside. Joe found records, neatly arranged and filed, of every aspect of the cardinal's work. He had meeting minutes written in black ink with a fountain pen in a beautiful flowing handwriting bordering on calligraphy going back for over twenty-five years. His records were beautiful to behold. Joe rifled through the pages of notes. He found no cross-outs or overwritten words.

Was it possible to be this meticulous? He must have copied them from a draft, thought Joe.

When Joe opened the center desk drawer, he found another cache of extravagance. There were over a dozen fountain pens, each one more expensive than the last. Gold barrels engraved with exquisite art. There were pens of ivory and burnished wood, antique pens, and modern designer pens. Each one had a custom, engraved gold nib and was filled with black indelible ink. Bottles of ink were stored in the side drawer along with polishing cloths.

At least this is something he used for work, thought Joe. *It makes my Skilcraft, government issue, black ballpoint seem rather pedestrian.*

Joe combed through the files for the rest of the day and almost until noon the following day. There was not much to report. Most of the writing was in Italian and Joe didn't know what he was looking for anyway. Each file looked like the last one he examined. Page after page of handwritten notes, meetings, and letters to church officials all over the world filled the aging folders. The responses to the letters were sometimes clipped to the original. Some of the letters were written in French or Spanish and a few in English. Joe studied those in great detail and used them as a Rosetta Stone for understanding the others. He found this job, like most, became repetitive and predictable. Letters requesting donations were answered with an explanation of why the funds were not available at this particular time and then there was the inevitable paragraph of encouragement and a short homily on having faith and using the resources at hand, etc., etc.

I think I could write these with a little practice, thought Joe. *Maybe I missed my calling.*

Joe looked at the ornate clock on the cardinal's desk and decided it was time to head upstairs for the meeting. He had looked at the clock hundreds of times this morning. It amused him to think about something he read years ago. You look at a clock to find out what time it isn't. You can look at your watch and immediately, if someone asks you what time it is, you will inevitably have to look again. You were not registering the time, but instead you were making sure it was not time for something to happen. Joe finally saw it was almost time for the meeting with the Pope. Joe left the office and climbed the stairs to the next floor to meet Cardinal O'Riley. He couldn't get used to calling him Patrick.

Cardinal O'Riley was standing in the hallway when Joe turned the corner from the stairwell. He motioned for Joe to hurry and knocked. Apparently, they had received an invitation to enter. Cardinal O'Riley opened the door and held it for Joe. The Pope was having his lunch at an ornate table. A serving cart with a polished silver soup tureen sat in the corner. He immediately began to rise to welcome his guests.

"Please do not stand up, your Holiness. We are very grateful for the opportunity to meet with you today. Forgive us for interrupting your lunch," said Cardinal O'Riley.

"It is not an inconvenience, Cardinal O'Riley. I appreciate your help. Please introduce me to Dr. McPherson. I have heard so much about him."

Joe stepped forward tentatively and bowed slightly, not knowing how to greet the Pope.

"This is Dr. Joseph McPherson, your Holiness. Joe was a parishioner of mine in Washington. He holds a doctorate in biology from one of the most respected universities in the United States and worked for twenty years at the Central Intelligence Agency. He is eminently qualified to help us and he is also a good Catholic boy."

"We are very fortunate to have your help, my son. Welcome to the Vatican. Is there anything we can do to make you more comfortable?"

"I am very pleased to meet you, your Holiness. This is an honor I never expected. I must inform you that Cardinal O'Riley has exaggerated my qualifications, but I assure you I will do everything in my power to help."

"I respect your humility, my son. I know you will be successful in finding the person who has tempted Cardinal Stancampiano and taken part of our most precious possessions. Now, let me show you what we are so concerned about."

The Pope rose and walked to the Raphael on the wall. He swung out the painting to reveal a safe and opened it on the first attempt at the combination. When the door opened, he backed away, and motioned for Cardinal O'Riley to remove the gold box. O'Riley placed it on the sideboard as the Pope unbuttoned the top buttons on his tunic and fumbled for the chain that held the key. He unlocked the box and stood aside.

"Cardinal O'Riley, would you please open it for me. I find this whole affair very disconcerting."

Cardinal O'Riley spread a clean white cloth on the sideboard, opened the box, and carefully removed the contents. The bloody cloth was still intact and the coarseness of the fabric weave indicated it was of ancient origin. The locks of hair were tied in linen rags. Joe could not wait to get his hands on the artifacts. He forgot about the presence of the Pope, pulled out a magnifying glass, and began to examine the relics.

After several minutes he turned to the Pope and asked, "May I take pictures, your Holiness?"

"I would appreciate it if you did not. As you know, only a very few people even know this exists. Photographs would provide yet another source of worry. You may make sketches if you desire. Please excuse me," said the Pope as he sat back down at his lunch. "I have a full schedule this afternoon."

Joe continued to examine the relics under the watchful eye of Cardinal O'Riley. The hair was in excellent condition. The bloodstains looked more like rust than blood, but it appeared they were undisturbed and the cloth was still intact.

"It appears there has been minimal exposure to sunlight," said Joe quietly as if talking to himself. "The cloth has become desiccated over the years, but not oxidized.

The DNA should be intact. It is amazing to see something two thousand years old in such good condition."

"Are you finished?" asked Cardinal O'Riley. "We have to go soon. His Holiness has an appointment."

"I have seen everything I need to see. Short of running some tests, I have to assume this material is in excellent biological condition. I assume I am not permitted to take samples?"

"Definitely not. We have agreed that nothing else ever leaves the possession of the Pope."

"Then I am finished with my examination. Do you want me to put everything away?" asked Joe.

"I will replace it," answered the Pope. "What are the chances someone could use this to make a clone?"

"I would have to say it is quite possible. The hair and blood appear to be remarkably well preserved. They have been protected from sunlight and never subjected to foreign contaminants as far as I can tell from my preliminary examination. They have probably been handled over the years, but I would assume they were treated with great respect," responded Joe. "If they did indeed fall into the hands of someone who intended to extract DNA samples, I would have to conclude there is a high probability they could be successful."

"That is too bad," said the Pope as he opened the door for Joe and Cardinal O'Riley to leave. "In any case, we must assume the worst. God help you find the person who has part of our precious relics."

CHAPTER 9

The next few days Joe toiled to read every scrap of paper he could find in Cardinal Stamcampiano's office and apartment. Cardinal O'Riley provided him with the services of a translator to help decipher the hand written letters and understand the jargon of the Church. In the evenings, Joe combed through the personal effects of Cardinal Stancampiano looking for a clue to the identity of his benefactor. Joe could not find anything that seemed out of the ordinary, though the meaning of ordinary had certainly changed for him in the last week. The fact that he was sifting through the papers of a recently deceased cardinal who had at one time been a candidate for Pope was incredulous and to think he might be searching for a man who desired to bring down the Catholic Church was almost unimaginable.

Joe knew something was missing from the collection of papers he was finding. At night when he tried to sleep, he kept turning it over in his mind. *There is nothing personal in these papers, nothing to define an existence, especially of a man who obviously had an appetite for the finer things of life. There had to be records for the purchase of the luxury items. Where did he keep his money? Where did he purchase these things? This man, Stancampiano, was meticulous in his work. He wrote every letter by hand, in indelible ink, and filed each one in neat rows of alphabetized folders.*

The next morning, Joe opened the office door and

decided to look at everything again and with new eyes. He closed and locked the door and pulled the guest chair into the entryway. He sat staring at the office, running his eyes over every inch.

"There must be something here," he said aloud. "Where is it?"

Joe paced around the room, looking at every piece of furniture repeatedly. Intellectually, he felt he hadn't missed anything, but he had to keep looking. Quitting wasn't an option.

Joe started talking aloud again, a habit he had developed when he was doing research. If he said something out loud, maybe it would trigger a new thought or an idea. It's like telling someone your problem and solving it yourself in the process.

"I am just missing it. I have looked at every file cabinet and every drawer in the desk," he said as he sat down behind the desk. *I have pulled out the drawers and looked behind them. I have pulled out the writing surfaces in the desk and looked for any evidence of hidden openings, keys, safes, maps, telephone numbers. I have done it again twice, and now three times. It is making me crazy. Think. Think. It must be here.*

Joe got up from the chair and began to walk around the room. He looked at the bookcases again. Beautiful antique carved oak with inlay. Museum pieces, no doubt. The posts that held the shelves were carved with vines entwined and leaves that protruded outwardly. Quite realistic. The books sat on thick shelves carved on the front surface and polished underneath. The finish had the patina only time and good care can bestow. The bases of the shelves were about three feet high and elaborately carved with biblical scenes. They were truly a work of art. The floral pattern surrounding the scenes on the front of the base formed the beginning of the vines that grew up the support posts.

Joe knelt down to look at the artwork and feel the smooth carving. As he caressed the designs, he noticed the front panel was slightly loose. At first, he assumed the wood had dried out and shrunk slightly, loosening the joints. Then he began to try to move the panel and to his surprise, he was able to push it inward about an inch in the center. When he released it, the panel popped open, revealing a rollout file drawer. Joe pushed in the other side of the panel and it too popped out revealing a two drawer, side-by-side file filled with carefully labeled manila folders. He greedily opened the closest one and knew he had found the missing files. Every illicit purchase was carefully documented. There were letters of inquiry, purchase orders, instructions, guaranties, and a few repair letters. Without standing up, Joe crawled over to the other large, matching bookcase and found it opened in a similar manner.

"Now, this is more like it," he said in self congratulation.

Joe spent the rest of the day combing through the files and cataloging the merchandise. He worked far into the night before he had a complete list of purchases. The total cost came to almost three million dollars. Cardinal Stancampiano had a very generous patron, indeed. Joe began to put the folders in chronological order. The purchases were filed according to type: watches, rosaries, suits, jewelry, etc., etc. He finally located the first purchase. The cardinal had purchased a gold crucifix in November of 1990. It had been eighteen years ago when the good cardinal had begun his spending spree. Dolly, the sheep, had not been born until July of 1996. This was more than four years before most of the world had any clue cloning was a possibility. Whoever was willing to offer millions of dollars for a sample of the Jesus Christ relics must have been very knowledgeable in the latest developments in the biological sciences.

I had just finished my Ph.D., thought Joe. *I knew it might be possible to clone a mammal, but I would not be willing to gamble that kind of money on the probability, even if I had it to gamble.*

Joe went to bed that night and slept soundly for the first time since he had arrived. He knew he had his first lead. Surely Cardinal Stancampiano would not wait long to spend his ill-gotten gains. The fact he bought a religious object first was telling. He clearly was feeling guilt. *He seemed to get past that, however,* Joe mused. *It didn't take long before he started buying really expensive and self-indulgent personal articles and clothing.*

After Joe had eaten breakfast in the cafeteria the next morning, he returned to Cardinal Stamcampiano's office and called Cardinal O'Riley.

"Can you come down for a few minutes?" Joe asked. "I think I have made some progress. I can tell you what he bought and when he bought it. I think we finally have something to work with."

"I'll be right down," answered Cardinal O'Riley.

Cardinal O'Riley, true to his word, entered almost immediately and sat across the desk from Joe. Joe, without speaking, handed O'Riley a manila folder. Inside, there were pages and pages listing expensive personal items, clothing, shoes, jewelry, museum pieces, rare books, expensive liquor and wines, and the occasional trip or cruise. The cardinal reviewed the list of purchases and prices for several minutes in silence. Finally, he sat back in his chair and looked at Joe.

"This was a man who definitely enjoyed the finer things in life," remarked Cardinal O'Riley, "and, not only that, he knew what they were. I have never heard of some of these brands. Where does a simple man of God learn how to spend this much money? Have you run a total?"

"As near as I can figure it, Cardinal, he has spent almost three million dollars over the last twenty years. Some of the money would have accumulated from interest. I also found a checkbook on a local bank and the bank statements. He still has more than one hundred thousand dollars in the local bank and there is also a folder for a Swiss bank account. I have that account number, but not the password. I think we will find more money there."

"How much do you think they paid Cardinal Stancampiano for the relics?"

"I would say on the order of two million dollars. Even though his purchases, at least the ones I know about, add up to quite a bit more than that. Interest on the accounts would add to the amount he had available. 'Compound interest is the most powerful force in the universe', to quote Dr. Einstein."

"Write down the account number for me," replied Cardinal O'Riley. "I will have the Swiss Guard find the password and the balance. The Swiss Guard has been with us for centuries. We have a special relationship. As soon as I explain that Cardinal Stancampiano has been embezzling from the Church, the bank will give us access to his account. At any rate, we have power of attorney to handle all of Stamcampiano's matters. It won't be a problem."

"Technically, he isn't embezzling, Cardinal. We really can't prove he has done anything wrong, including taking the relics."

"Don't be a fool, Joe. Stancampiano wasn't a rich man. He was from a poor family and no one has a patron that generous. He stole from the Church and he sold something priceless. Until we find out who he sold it to and what they intend to do with it, we have to assume the worst. Now, a question for you. Do you really think is it possible to clone a person from the relics? You saw their condition and know the age. What are the odds?"

"I have been thinking about it a lot since the meeting with the Pope. I am not sure about the blood. Bacteria and fungi usually contaminate blood, like the rest of human remains. Almost as soon as we die, the bacteria in our bodies begins to break down cell tissue. However, this blood soaked into the linen garment and dried out quickly, I assume. I can also assume the humidity was extremely low due the climate in that region and the blood quickly desiccated.

"So you think a clone can be produced from the blood samples?"

"Maybe," responded Joe. "It could be possible. The Egyptians removed the internal organs immediately after death and placed them in a jar. This, combined with the use of salt and other preserving agents, prevented the bodies from decaying. We know from studies of Egyptian mummies, this procedure can preserve human remains for thousands of years.

However, more likely, one would try to use the hair samples."

"Why so?" asked O'Riley.

"Hair follicles preserve DNA," continued Joe, "because of the plastic-like protection the hair material affords. Hair is almost like nature's way of packaging the genome in a protective wrapping. Since we don't know how much hair was originally saved, we can't estimate how many samples were taken. They could have hundreds or even thousands of hair samples. That would be enough to experiment with for years."

The cardinal rubbed his chin, solemnly shook his head from side to side, and looked into space as if lost in thought. Finally, he asked, "Where do we go from here, Joe?"

"First, I need to know who came to see Cardinal Stancampiano in the weeks and months before he started spending money. We have a start date from the receipts. Do you keep records of visitors?"

Cardinal O'Riley chuckled, "Do we keep records? Do we keep records? Joe, if we don't do anything else right around here, we keep records. We have catacombs full of records. We send records to caves for storage. We have a record of everything that has happened in the Church for over two thousand years. Every visitor that comes into the Vatican must sign in and out. I will admit, however, you were the exception. You are not officially here."

"Sounds like a Catch-22 in the making," responded Joe. "I just hope I am not unfortunate enough to disappear while I'm here like that character of Joseph Heller's, Captain Yossarian. He was killed on a bombing mission before he was officially signed in. He couldn't be listed as deceased because he was never formally processed onto the base and thus couldn't have gone on a mission."

"We intend to take good care of you, Joe. The Church takes good care of its own."

"I am thankful for that, Cardinal. When can I get the sign-in sheets?"

"I will call the commandant today. I will expedite them. We will have the rest of Cardinal Stancampiano's money transferred to my special account to investigate this case. It seems only fitting that we can use the thief's money to catch him."

"We haven't caught him yet, Cardinal. Let me know as soon as we have the visitation records. I am going to take a walk around the Vatican grounds. I haven't seen the sun since I arrived."

"We will catch him, Joe. Mark my words. Nothing can be allowed to bring down the Church. The Church must live on no matter what else happens in this world. It is written in the Book of Revelation that Jesus Christ will return and he will raise the dead, those who have been believers. We will have the last judgment. The martyrs of the Church will be rewarded. God is working through us to fulfill His prophecies."

"I'll take your word for that, Cardinal. Right now, my job is to find out who took the property of the Church and try to get it back. If you will excuse me, I think I need time to rest and think."

Two days later the Swiss Guard brought in a microfiche reader and a box of dusty plastic squares that contained the sign-in sheets for the last twenty-five years.

"I'm sorry, Dr. McPherson, but we are still in the

Stone Age around here. We scan in the sheets now and create PDF files that are on-line. This new procedure was only started about two or three years ago. All of the older records were put on microfiche and stored in the repository caves. The sign-in records are rarely, if ever, requested and we don't plan to convert them to digital images."

"This will do fine," responded Joe. "Just put the reader on the desk and leave the box here on the floor. It will take some time to go through them, but I don't think I will have to look at all of them."

CHAPTER 10

For the next few days, Joe viewed visitor records for ten hours a day. Unfortunately, the records were for all Swiss Guard stations and there were about twenty locations at that time for visitor's entry. Joe soon found Cardinal Stancampiano had very few visitors. He scanned the sheets looking for the unmistakable name of Cardinal Stancampiano under the person to be visited column. He started with the date Stancampiano ordered the crucifix and went back, day by day, looking for visitors. He made a list of visitors and the date and time of each visit. The first month before the date of the crucifix, the cardinal had only ten visitors. Joe decided to keep going. The second month before, Stancampiano had twelve visitors. *Now I have twenty-two, but three are repeaters.*

I can probably eliminate the repeat visitors, thought Joe. *Once you come for the treasure, why take a chance on being caught? On the other hand, maybe I come here once to get the lay of the land, and then come back for the actual break-in. What am I going to do with this list? Most of these people are probably good, Christian people and they had a legitimate reason for coming. What am I looking for?*

Joe continued to search through the names, looking for something that would be an anomaly. *Is there something different about an entry that stands out from the rest?* Finally, he saw something that intrigued him. *There was a sign-*

in at five fifty-six in the afternoon. The handwriting was distinctive.

Then Mr. Chevalier signed out at five fifty-nine. The odd thing was Joe recognized the handwriting of Cardinal Stancampiano. The cardinal had personally signed out this visitor. The penmanship, bordering on calligraphy and with a broad nib fountain pen and black ink, was unmistakable. Nothing else on the sign-in sheet was even close.

"Why did the cardinal sign out this particular visitor?" Joe mused aloud. *He only stayed for three minutes, assuming their watches were synchronized. I'd bet on the good cardinal having the correct time. If he says it is 5:59, then it was 5:59.*

Joe copied the signature of the visitor who also had excellent handwriting. *Not that common,* thought Joe. *Now that everyone uses the computer for correspondence, the art of writing is almost passé.*

The name intrigued Joe. He turned it repeatedly in his mind. Chevalier. He remembered the French actor, Maurice Chevalier. He had seen the movie *Gigi* with Leslie Caron years ago. He remembered thinking at the time this old dude was more than a little strange with his preoccupation for a pubescent girl. *Just another dirty old man,* he remembered thinking.

The first name, Ramptet, was a new one to Joe. *I never heard of anyone named Ramptet. Must be a rare French name. Maybe a family sir name.*

Joe took a sheet of paper from the drawer and a fountain pen from Cardinal Stancampiano's desk set. He painstakingly attempted to copy the signature displayed on the microfiche reader as accurately as possible. Then Joe picked up the phone and dialed Cardinal O'Riley's extension.

"May I speak to the Cardinal?" he asked. "Thank you. I will hold. Hello, Cardinal. Joe here. I need to use the internet. I think I have a lead. How long will it take you to assemble the Task Force?"

"I will call the library," Cardinal O'Riley responded. "You will have internet access by the time you can walk there. How soon do you need to see us?"

"Tomorrow morning would be soon enough. How about nine?"

"We will be in the second floor conference room. See you then. Joe, I hope you have something good for us."

"I don't know if you will think it is good or not, but I think you will find it interesting."

Joe hung up the phone and looked around the room. He spotted Cardinal Stancampiano's briefcase sitting by the bookcase, opened it, and slid his research documents across the desk into it. He opened the top drawer and selected a gold Mont Blanc and a sterling silver Tiffany pen from Stancampiano's collection. He opened both making sure they were full of ink and then placed them carefully in his shirt pocket.

"It sure is easy to get used to having the best," he said aloud to himself.

Joe grabbed the briefcase and headed for the library.

CHAPTER 11

When Joe walked into the conference room the next day the cardinal task force was seated and waiting for him.

Cardinal Sanchez stood and held out his hand.

"Good to see you again, Joe. Can I make you a cup of cappuccino?"

Joe blushed and shook his head no. He bowed slightly to each of the cardinals. He sat down at the head of the conference table and waited for Cardinal O'Riley to start the meeting.

Cardinal O'Riley allowed sufficient time to pass so he would be the center of attention. He was a master at taking charge of any meeting and he did it deliberately and instinctively.

"Joe has informed me he has made some progress in determining the perpetrator of this heinous crime and we are here to listen. Joe, the floor is yours."

Joe stood and walked to the front of the room.

"Gentlemen, or rather your Eminences, I believe I have found something I must bring to you for your consideration. As you all know, this is a very cold trail and we don't have much to go on. I have to assume Cardinal Stancampiano did not want anyone to find out about his disloyalty. I have had to look for anything that is anomalous."

"First, I discovered secret files in the cardinal's office that contained records of purchases of many extraordinary expensive items he acquired over the past twenty years.

He bought things that are far beyond the reach of most of us. The total value of these items amounts to almost three million dollars," Joe paused for effect.

"I catalogued each receipt and put them in chronological order. The first of his expensive items was purchased in early 1990. I assumed he would not wait long before he started spending money, so I asked for the visitor sign-in sheets from 1988 through 1990. I started going through them day by day. I have to tell you I had no idea what to look for, but hoped to would find a clue."

Joe sensed his audience was getting bored. *Too bad*, he thought. *I sweated blood to get this far and they are going to have to let me tell the story my way.*

"I made a copy of this page," continued Joe as he handed several sheets of paper to Cardinal O'Riley and indicated for him to distribute them.

"A visitor signed in to see Cardinal Stancampiano at 5:56 in the afternoon. He signed out at 5:59. What is interesting about this particular visitor, notwithstanding he only stayed three minutes is he was signed out by Cardinal Stancampiano. I believe that is his handwriting. Do you agree with me?"

The assembled cardinals examined the signature page and nodded agreement the sign-out was indeed in the handwriting of Cardinal Stancampiano. Cardinal O'Riley nodded for Joe to continue.

"The signature is somewhat difficult to read, but I interpreted it to be 'Ramptet Chevalier'. I spent considerable time on the internet yesterday researching the name. First, I could not find a person who had such a name. Wikipedia provides about thirteen different definitions of the word Chevalier. I would assume you all know chevalier is a

French word meaning, literally, 'horseman', but used as a title, it is the equivalent of the English 'knight'."

"Interestingly, the thirteenth definition provided on Wikipedia is 'the title used by Knights Templar'."

"Surely, the Knights Templar are not involved in this," interrupted Cardinal O'Riley. "They haven't been heard of for hundreds of years."

"Hear me out, Cardinal. I have more," said Joe as he continued. "As I was reading the article on chevalier, I began to doodle with the name Ramptet. If chevalier was a knight, then what was a Ramptet? I looked at the signature again. If you look carefully at the sign-in sheet, the first 'T' could be an 'L'. Then, with a little rearranging, the name Ramplet can be shown to be an anagram for Templar. This visitor left his calling card. He is from the Knights Templar."

Something closely akin to pandemonium broke out in the room. Several languages were being spoken. The cardinals were all talking simultaneously and no one was listening. Joe allowed the din to play out and then he cleared his throat.

"Would you like to hear the rest?"

Silence answered his question.

"I'm sure all of you know this story better than I, but I will repeat it anyway. As you probably know, the Crusaders from Europe succeeded in capturing Jerusalem from the Moslems in 1099, only 33 years after the invasion of England by William the Conqueror. As soon as the city was captured, many Christians attempted to make the pilgrimage to Jerusalem to visit the Holy Lands. However, there were bandits and roving Arab tribes along the route and many of the faithful were slaughtered and even the lucky ones were robbed. After about twenty years of losing many faithful and dedicated followers, two knights from the time of the Crusades proposed a monastic order that would dedicate themselves to the protection of pilgrims attempting to make the journey to Jerusalem. In 1129, the Catholic Church officially endorsed the Order. Because of their dedication in protecting pilgrims bound for the Holy Lands, the Templars soon became a favorite charity of the wealthy and received money, land, businesses, and noble-born sons."

Joe paused again for effect then continued, "The Knights Templar received another huge benefit from the Church in 1139. Pope Innocent II exempted the order from obedience to local laws. His ruling meant the Templars could pass freely through all borders, were not required to pay any taxes, and were exempt from all authority except that of the Pope. They were initially so poor their coat of arms shows two knights riding one horse. This symbol is still used to remind them of their humble beginnings. However, they did not stay poor long. They developed into a powerful organization with roots in Europe and throughout the Middle East. They even invented a banking system allowing travelers to deposit funds in Europe and reclaim them when they reached Jerusalem. That greatly reduced robbery along the routes."

"Where is this going, Joe? I hope you didn't come here to give us a history lesson," interrupted Cardinal O'Riley.

"Bear with me, your Eminence. I think you will see the connection soon," Joe continued. "I also discovered a couple of other interesting facts. First, they were known as the Knights Templar because King Baldwin II of Jerusalem agreed to give them space for a headquarters on the Temple Mount, in the captured Al Aqsa Mosque. The Temple Mount was surrounded by mystique. It was built on what is believed to be the ruins of the Temple of Solomon. The Crusaders therefore referred to the Al Aqsa Mosque as Solomon's Temple. You will see how this is important to our current situation."

"So," continued Joe, "the Christians held Jerusalem for almost a hundred years, from 1099 to 1187 when it was recaptured by Saladin's forces. By this time, the Knights Templar were a powerful and wealthy order. The Templar Order, though its members were sworn to individual poverty, gained control of wealth beyond direct donations. For example, a nobleman who was interested in participating in the Crusades might place all his assets under Templar management while he was away. Of course, if he did not return, the Knights Templar would continue to control his lands. In this way, they became extremely powerful."

"At any rate," continued Joe, "the Crusaders retook Jerusalem in 1229 and held it until 1244 when the Turks captured it. During this second occupation by the Christians, the Knights Templar returned to Jerusalem, but did not participate in defending the city. It seems they were preoccupied with excavating the ruins beneath the temple."

"And what were they looking for?" asked Cardinal Sanchez.

"This is a point of much discussion," responded Joe. "Some think they were looking for the Holy Grail. There are rumors it was buried in tunnels below Solomon's Temple. Others think they were looking for the Ark of the Covenant. I believe they were looking for the relics of Jesus Christ."

"But do you have any proof?" injected Cardinal O'Riley. "This just seems like wild speculation to me. So far I don't see the connection."

Joe walked to the white board and wrote 1229 to 1244. "These are the years the Christians held Jerusalem the second time we captured it. The Knights Templar abandoned the temple in 1240. Every man left at the same time, returning to Europe by way of Rome. They left four years before the Turks recaptured the city."

"And what does that prove?" asked Cardinal O'Riley.

"I think the reason they left was because they found what they were looking for. They spent the years from 1229 to 1240, eleven years, excavating beneath the ruins of the temple. Then they abruptly left and never returned. Further, they went straight to Rome and had an audience with the Pope. Did they deliver the relics? I think they did."

"What proof do you have the Templars actually found the sacred relics?" asked Cardinal O'Riley. "Why would they be buried under the temple?"

"Where else would the early Christians hide anything that valuable?" responded Joe. "They were not wealthy and did not own anything that could be defended. They were primarily from Jewish backgrounds. Jesus was a Jewish Rabbi. The Temple of Solomon was the last great stronghold of the Jews. Why not hide them there? They knew the Romans would try to destroy any remnants of Jesus if they could."

"And now, the interesting part," continued Joe. "The Knights Templar continued to flourish. They became even richer and more powerful. In fact, they almost single-handedly financed the Hundred Years War for King Phillip IV of France. By the end of the war, he was deeply indebted to them. Phillip convinced Pope Clement V to support him against the Templars. The Pope issued a papal bull instructing the Christian monarchs throughout Europe to arrest all Templars and seize their assets. On Friday, October 13, 1307, King Philip ordered scores of French Templars to be simultaneously arrested. He held hearings to determine the Templars' guilt or innocence. The Templars were charged with idolatry, heresy, obscene rituals and homosexuality, financial corruption, fraud, and secrecy among other things. Many Templars were tortured into confessing. The bottom line is scores of Knights Templar were burned at the stake."

"There you have it. That is my theory. The Knights Templar certainly had motive. We know they survived the inquisition begun by Clement V. They continued to prosper in Spain and other countries. They went underground to avoid the wrath of the Church, but they were too well established to be obliterated. They had the means to survive and I assume they never forgave the Church. They had opportunity. They knew of the relics. They had the means to pay a bribe to get what they wanted. Motive, opportunity, means; that usually results in guilt."

"Do you have anything else to support this theory, Joe?" asked Cardinal Sanchez.

"Not really. I do find it very interesting this visitor arrived on Friday, October 13, 1989. This is the only Friday the 13th that occurs in October for about five years during this time period. Friday, October 13 in the year 1307 was the date the Templars were seized. I don't think this is a coincidence. The man who took the relics was exceedingly deliberate in his preparations and he left his calling card. These Templar folks apparently know how to hold a grudge."

Cardinal O'Riley stood up to signify the end of the meeting.

"Cardinal O'Riley, please grant me a moment," spoke Cardinal Wygonik in a heavily accented voice. "As you all know, my English is not nearly as good as my Polish, but I have been listening very carefully to Dr. McPherson and his theory. It seems to me he very well could be correct. The Church made a grave error when they allowed the Templar Order to be sacrificed for expediency. The Templars were punished for being successful. We have always assumed the twelve chosen cardinals were the only mortals that knew about the sacred relics. Now, it appears this information may have been passed down by the Templars for these hundreds of years. Why should we assume they intend to use them to destroy the Church? We have been neither threatened nor extorted. It has been over twenty years now and we have not heard from them. Has it occurred to you they might believe they have a right to possess these sacred relics? If Dr. McPherson is correct, they searched for many years to find them in the ruins of the Temple of Solomon. They brought them to the Pope as a gift and their ultimate reward was to be thrown to the wolves of Europe. Even I might find it difficult to forgive such a travesty if someone caused my companions to be burned at the stake for no good reason. I think we must keep an open mind. We should look to God for guidance and pray we resolve this in a Christian manner. One cannot always understand how God works. I will be praying for you Dr. McPherson."

"Thank you, your Eminence. I appreciate your prayers," replied Joe.

Cardinal O'Riley quickly rose to cut off further discussion.

"What we do now?" he asked Joe. "Assuming you are correct, how do we find this Templar?"

"I wish I knew," answered Joe. "I am going to have to think about this for a while. I will sleep on it and hope I get an inspiration. That, your Eminences, concludes my presentation. You now know everything I know and probably a lot more. If you get any ideas, I would greatly appreciate a call."

"Thank you Joe. I will walk out with you," said Cardinal O'Riley as he held the door to the conference room for Joe to exit. "What is your next step?"

"I need a computer, Cardinal. I think I will take a taxi and look for a good electronics store. Can I get internet connections in my room and office?"

"I have no idea," answered O'Riley. "I have never learned how to use a computer. I think I can make it happen, though. We are counting on you, Joe. I think you are right about the Knights Templar. It scares me to think there are the forces of darkness out there trying to destroy the Church. Be very careful, Joe. These people could be dangerous. Why don't I call you a driver? That is why we have all these limousines."

"No thanks. I need to get away from everything for a few hours, Cardinal. I will be more comfortable alone. I have always needed time to think and I don't need company for that. I will be back later today. If you could look into the internet connections while I'm gone, I would appreciate it. See you later."

CHAPTER 12

Joe stopped by his office and picked up Cardinal Stancampiano's briefcase on the way out. When he stepped into the sunshine, he felt a weight lift from his shoulders. He headed for the taxi stand and soon was on his way to downtown Rome.

The taxi driver spoke just enough English to grasp that Joe was looking for a computer store and soon they melded into traffic. Joe had never been to Rome and, so far, all he had seen was the inside of the Vatican. He asked the driver if they were far from the Coliseum. Since the driver was on the meter, he made a couple of quick turns and soon they were driving by the site of the Roman games. Joe turned from window to window and watched the scenery as the taxi wound through narrow streets.

"How about the Trevi Fountain? The Spanish Steps?" Joe kept asking and the driver gladly complied. Finally, tired of sightseeing from the inside of a taxi, Joe stopped at a computer store.

"Do you want I should wait?" asked the driver.

"Sure," answered Joe. "I don't think I will be too long."

The store was full of interesting gadgets. Like most scientists, Joe was enamored with electronic devices, especially those that were useful for work. For the first time in his life, he could buy the things he really wanted without regard to price. It had always been a compromise, the most capability for the least money. Now he could get the best. He had discovered what remained of Stancampiano's bribe in the Swiss bank. O'Riley, true to his word, had no trouble transferring it to the special account they had established for the investigation. Joe was flush for the first time in his life.

He found a laptop that would run almost forever on batteries. It was packed with memory and contained a huge hard drive. Joe had the sales clerk take it to checkout and went to the cell phone department. He found an international phone and bought a usage plan with unlimited minutes. His new American Express card was very useful.

The taxi driver, having successfully fended off both police and irate drivers, was still double-parked outside. Joe climbed into the aging Fiat.

"Where to now, sir?"

"How about a good wine store?"

"No problem. We have many of those in Rome. Should we head back toward the Vatican?"

"That would be a good idea. Just stop somewhere along the way back."

"No problem."

Joe found a good bottle of Merlot in the small shop. He was about to pay when he decided he might as well get two, one for tomorrow night. The driver returned to the Vatican in record time. Joe passed through security and headed back to his room.

He emptied the contents of Stancampiano's briefcase on the bed. He admired his new computer and cell phone. He realized he was the only person who knew the number.

No calls tonight, he thought as he smiled. *I was not getting that many calls on my other phone, come to think about it.*

Joe looked around the room for a corkscrew. He had seen one somewhere. He remembered it was in the top bureau drawer. Naturally, it was inlayed and probably worth hundreds of dollars. Stancampiano never sent a boy to do a man's job. Joe opened a bottle of Merlot.

Nice glasses, he thought as he filled the gold-rimmed glass. *Probably from Murano.*

Joe plugged the computer into the wall and turned it on.

Always use the charger, he remembered, *until the battery in fully charged the first time. I must remember to get a plug adapter if I travel. This European design won't work in most countries.*

Joe took the cell phone out of the package and started charging it. He took another sip of wine and refilled his glass. *This is good stuff. It goes down easy.*

Joe sat at his desk and started experimenting with the new computer. The internet connection worked and soon he was on line. Joe lost track of time and when he reached over to pour another glass of wine, he discovered the bottle was empty. Where had he left the other bottle? It was still in his briefcase, actually Stancampiano's briefcase, but, after all, Cardinal Stancampiano wouldn't be needing it any more. Joe got up and walked to the bed to retrieve the wine.

I really should wait until tomorrow to drink this second bottle, he thought. *But, on the other hand, I deserve to celebrate for finding out about the Knights Templar.*

"A little reward is in order," he said aloud to himself.

Joe reached for the wine and as he lifted it out of the briefcase, the light from the bed lamp cast a shadow inside the case. At first, it didn't register, then Joe realized the leather in the bottom of the briefcase had a rather strange pattern worn into it. Straight lines that formed rectangles crisscrossed the soft leather lining. He hadn't noticed them before. Joe set the bottle of wine on the desk and moved his computer to one side. He set the briefcase on the desk and held the lamp at an angle to highlight the indentations in the leather. He opened the desk drawer and found a straight edge. Using a pencil, he traced the lines lightly. There was definitely a pattern. Joe walked to the bathroom and got his wallet. He pulled out a dollar bill and measured it against the rectangle.

This is the briefcase used to deliver the money. There is no doubt, but the bills were certainly not dollars, thought Joe. *They were at least hundreds, maybe larger.*

CHAPTER 13

When Joe awoke the next morning, his head was pounding.

Damn, he thought, *I forgot how much you have to pay for the night before. Red wine is the worst. I should have stopped with the first bottle but, hell; I've been saying that for twenty years. 'Drink till it's gone', that's my motto.*

Joe turned on the water in the shower and let it heat up while he brushed his teeth. He stood in the shower for the next twenty minutes and let the warm water run over his head.

There has to be something primeval about warm water running over you. Even baboons like to sit in natural hot springs. Maybe it's because we spend the first nine months of our existence in a wet womb at a constant temperature of 98.6 degrees. Why do I always think of crazy stuff like this when I have a hangover?

When he finally felt good enough to dry off, he shaved, and put on his clothes. The cleaning people had been taking his laundry and returning his shirts and pants to the closet, freshly starched and pressed.

"Not a bad life," he judged.

Now, where was I when I was so rudely interrupted by drinking wine? Oh yes, I have discovered the bagman's bag. Will my theory still hold in the light of day?

Joe sat down at the desk and looked carefully at the inside of the briefcase again. The markings in the suede leather lining of the case clearly had been imprinted with the grid-like pattern that had the exact dimensions of American currency.

No wonder this case didn't have the usual built-in penholders and a portfolio for storing papers. Just a rectangular box, albeit a very nice box. This case is plain, but elegant. The workmanship is excellent. Even though it is twenty years old, it's still in great condition. Some things, like class, just don't go out of style.

There was a simple logo sewn to the inside lining. Joe had never heard of Lobb. He booted up his computer as he continued to inspect the case. He Googled Lobb and immediately he knew he had a lead.

John Lobb Bootmaker was located on St. James Street, London. The firm was well over a hundred years old. The shop was frequented by royalty and gentlemen of London. Where else would a gentleman have a case specially built for such an important purpose? If you are going to wait centuries to reclaim your property, or at least part of it, you might want an elegant case for carrying the bribe.

Joe picked up the phone and dialed Cardinal O'Riley's number.

"Good morning, Cardinal. Doing well, thanks for asking. I believe I had a breakthrough last night. I think I'm on to something. Yes, I'm pretty sure. This could be the break we have been looking for. I have to go to London to follow up. Hold your questions for now. I will be up to tell you all about it just as soon as I get some breakfast. See you then."

As luck would have it, Alitalia was not on strike that day and by nightfall; Joe was aboard a flight to London, Heathrow.

CHAPTER 14

Joe found a taxi as soon as he exited Heathrow.

"Do you know a good hotel?" Joe asked the driver as he stashed his bags in what should have been the driver's side of the black taxi.

"I know all the hotels, governor, good and bad. Where are you going? Business or pleasure? Cheap or expensive?"

"I'm going to St. James Place tomorrow. I am looking for a leather shop. John Lobb. You know it?"

"I know of it all right. I hope you have deep pockets, governor. How about the Rubens? It is not far from the Royal Mews and Victoria Station. Buckingham Palace Park is only a couple of blocks. I'd say you'll like the Rubens."

"I'll take your word for it."

The Rubens at the Palace was a holdover from the Victorian age. The liveried greeters, in their regimental blue coats with gold epaulets, grabbed his suitcase from the front of the cab before Joe could open the rear door and pay the driver. Joe was somewhat stunned at the amount of the cab fare from Heathrow, but he shrugged, it was after all, money transferred from Cardinal Stancampiano's secret account.

The hotel lobby was paneled in rich mahogany, reminiscent of the proverbial old boys clubs. It exuded an air of elegance slightly down at the heel. The brass-adorned elevators were gleaming, but the residue of polish at the edges spoke of many years of use. Reception was busy, but after a short wait, Joe was presenting his passport and proffering the American Express card to the clerk. She was the model of crisp efficiency and her British accent was refreshing yet slightly intimidating. Her precise use of the language made Joe reflect on how much he relied on colloquialisms and hackneyed phrases when he talked. He was almost mesmerized by the time she pointed to the 'lift' and handed him the piece of plastic that served as his room key.

Joe waved off the bellhop and boarded the elevator with his roll-on and the cardinal's briefcase.

I wonder if I will ever go back to the Vatican? he thought as the lift stopped at the third floor. *I am carrying everything I own in the world. It is a relief not to have anything. No responsibility and no commitment. I am even having fun again. I don't know how long this will last, but for now, it's good.*

The room was pleasant and had a decent view of Buckingham Palace Road.

The days are really long here at this time of year. I wonder what time it gets dark? I can't recall the latitude of England; about fifty degrees north if I remember correctly, over half way to the North Pole.

Joe unpacked his shaving kit and turned on the TV. He watched BBC1 until he fell asleep. The sun was streaming through his window when he awoke, still on top of the covers and fully dressed. He looked at his watch.

Five o'clock in the morning and I am fully awake. It must be the time difference between here and Rome.

After a quick shower and a change of clothes, Joe headed down to the lobby.

"Good morning, sir. You are up bright and early today," said the desk clerk. "We have coffee and tea in the Palace Lounge. Kindly help yourself."

"Thank you," responded Joe. "How do I get to the park from here? I feel like a walk this morning."

"Just turn right out of the front door and it is only about two blocks. You will see the Mews on your left. Sir, you should carry an umbrella. You may use one of ours there by the door. It is supposed to rain later this morning. This has been a dreary and cold summer. It rains most every day."

Armed with an umbrella that served as a walking stick and a cup of hot coffee, Joe strode out of the hotel lobby and down the street toward the Royal Mews. The cool damp summer air felt good as he walked briskly into St. James Park. There were a few joggers and the occasional early riser sitting on a bench, but for the most part, he had the park to himself. A particularly shapely jogger ran past Joe.

I hope they don't have as many muggers here as we do in D.C. I sure wouldn't want my wife running on the National Mall when it's this deserted.

He could see Buckingham Palace in the distance and decided to walk toward it. As he approached the Palace, he noticed the Palace Guards.

I wonder where they get those bearskin hats? I would think the animal activists would be all over that. The Queen must be in residence. The royal flag is flying over the Palace.

Joe walked through the Victoria Memorial and decided to head over to the Green Park Underground station. The giant sycamore trees were flush with large green leaves that would soon turn brown and litter the landscape.

These guys must be well over a hundred years old, thought Joe as he walked beneath the outstretched limbs. He could faintly hear Big Ben ringing out the half hour. *There is something stately and permanent about England. It is as if it has always existed. They have museums hundreds of years older than the United States. England has been overrun, but never conquered. William the Conqueror ruled the place, but they don't speak French. The English always persevered by sheer determination and unwillingness to change in spite of who lived in the castles. The Empire waxed and waned, but left an indelible mark on the world as no other nation. The language of the world is English. Not too bad for an island country with few natural resources.*

As he walked down the steps into the Green Park Underground, Joe bought a paper and found a bakery with fresh croissants. He savored his breakfast as he read the tabloid. It was after nine before Joe returned to the Rubens. Clouds had covered the sky and a light drizzle was falling.

When Joe walked into John Lobb Bootmaker later that morning, his senses were overwhelmed by the smell of new leather and displays of incredibly beautiful boots and shoes. The gentleman behind the counter nodded to Joe to assure him that he knew Joe was waiting and then turned his undivided attention back to the customer at the counter. Both men were dressed impeccably. Joe would not have known the buyer from the seller except for their behavior. The client was looking through a brochure and trying to decide which style he preferred. After a lengthy discussion about how the boots would be used, the customer finally decided.

"How long until they are completed?" he asked.

"We are backlogged at the present.," responded the salesman. "Unfortunately, it will be at least six weeks, sir, before we can begin working on them. I assume there has not been any change in your size requirement?"

"I am still the same size through the foot, though I have apparently been experiencing some upward migration of my other dimensions. I attribute it to closet shrinkage. My man hangs my trousers and the next time I put them on, they have shrunk perceptively. Have you anything that would prevent such untoward behavior?"

"If we could develop such a product, I think we would find an excellent market. I will ring you when we get the preliminary lasting sewn and you can come in for a fitting."

"Very well," said the customer. "I shall be looking forward to getting them well before hunt season."

"We will do our utmost. Thank you for your business, Lord Randall."

"May I help you?" said the clerk as Lord Randall left the shop.

"I have a rather strange request, I'm afraid," responded Joe as he set the case on the counter. "This case was owned by a member of our firm who recently died. I have taken his position and I would like to purchase a new one of the same dimensions. While this case is still in reasonably good condition, I am somewhat superstitious, I suppose. The case has your label inside and, since I was passing through London, I decided to inquire about buying a new one."

"Let me take a closer look," said the clerk. "We don't, as a rule, make attaché cases. Most of our business is in custom boots and shoes. Hmmm, this is an old one. It's ours all right. This is our logotype. Sometimes we get counterfeit merchandise. They never get the tag right. This logo is real, however. The case was made right here in this shop. We haven't used that brand of hinge for over ten years. The size is rather strange as well," said the clerk, measuring the case with a yellow cloth tape measure he pulled from his vest pocket. "I have never seen anything just like it. Do you have a few minutes? I have someone here who might be able to remember this particular case."

"I am in no hurry. Take as much time as you need."

The salesman picked up the phone and dialed what must have been an extension since there were too few numbers for an outside call.

"Higgins, can you come up to the front desk? I have something I want to show you."

A few moments later a short, stocky man emerged from a door in the back of the room. He was wearing a well-used leather apron with tools hanging out of the pockets. His hands were rough and dye stained, and the prominent muscles and veins in his wrists and forearms attested to years of hard use. He wore rimless glasses and had a shock of white hair that fell down across his forehead.

"Higgins, this gentleman would like to know if you can remember anything about this case," said the shopkeeper, who then excused himself to wait on the next customer.

Higgins raised his head slightly to look though the bottom lens of his bifocals and began an intense inspection of the case. He grunted a few times as he turned it over and looked at every surface and joint.

Finally, he said, "I made this case about twenty years ago. I remember it distinctly. Why do you want to know?" looking directly at Joe.

Joe repeated his story with as much conviction as he could muster. Higgins listened politely, but Joe could tell he was not convinced.

"What do you remember about the man who had it made?"

"I can't say as how I remember much of anything, mate. It's been twenty year or more. I'll 'ave to think on it. Do you want me to make another one? That's special leather, you know. I 'ad an 'ell of a time getting it."

"I need to think on it, too," responded Joe. "Here is the number for my hotel and my cell phone number. If you remember something, give me a call. I would greatly appreciate your help."

"I'll see what I can do, mate. You got me curiosity up now. I'll check me files and see if I can find anything."

"Thanks, Mr. Higgins. I sure hope to hear from you," said Joe as he turned around and left the shop. The shopkeeper didn't look up as he was busy taking an order from a regular customer.

It was almost eight that evening when Joe's cell phone rang.

"Yes," said Joe into the phone. "I can find it. I'll meet you there at nine sharp."

CHAPTER 15

The taxi dropped Joe on Curzon Street and he walked the short block down to the Kings Arms. As he entered the pub, Joe saw the staircase to the second floor, just as Higgins had described. Joe climbed the worn and creaking wooden stairs and entered a dimly lit barroom that smelled of strong cigarettes and stale beer. He saw a refrigerated show case of pub food in the corner and a long oak bar with a heavy brass rung along the bottom. At least a dozen colorful tap handles lined the backside of the bar. Garish neon signs, blurred by the smoky atmosphere, proclaimed the availability of Guinness, Stella and numerous other brands Joe did not recognize. The room was crowded with mostly male revelers. The noise level was almost to the shouting stage, with ancient pinball games adding to the cacophony.

Joe stood at the top of the stairs until his eyes became accustomed to the dim light. Finally, he spotted Higgins at a small table overlooking Shepherd Market Square. Higgins was wearing an old tweed jacket, dark pants, and a flat driving cap, unsnapped in front, that covered his white hair. He was watching Joe and when he saw that Joe recognized him, he nodded toward the empty chair.

"Thanks for coming, Mr. Higgins," said Joe as he sat down at the ancient table.

"I assume you are willing to pay for information?" said Higgins. "I'm taking a chance meetin' you, you know. We ain't allowed to talk to customers. I guess they don't want us freelancin'."

Joe slid a hundred pound note across the table, hidden under his hand.

"This is for coming. If I get what I want, I will double that."

"Fair enough, gov. What do you want to know?"

A waiter interrupted the conversation and Joe ordered a pint of Guinness.

"When did you make the leather briefcase? What did the man look like that bought it? Do you know his name?"

"Hold your horses, gov. One question at a time. This gentleman come into the shop the summer of '89. He wanted a case made to his exact measurements. He was tall, light hair if I remember right, and he looked like a military man. He stood straight and had that walk like he had been in the military. I spent four years in the Royal Navy meself and I know that look. I took him for an officer, but he never said nothin' about it, so I didn't either."

"How old was he?"

"I'd say he was early thirties, maybe forty tops. Nice looking guy, 'e was."

"Did he say why he wanted the briefcase?"

"He said it was a samples case, but I never did believe that. When it left the shop, it had dividers in it. They were made out of harness leather and fit together with matching slots. They stood up in there like an egg carton. I made 'em myself. They were double stitched and polished to a shine."

"I saw their imprint in the lining. I couldn't find them.

They must have been discarded later. Do you remember the customer's name?"

"He said his name was Mr. Smith. I never did believe that either. Paid cash, he did. Half down and half when I finished. A pretty penny, too, it was. I wish I could have kept it all for meself."

The waiter returned with the Guinness. Joe put a ten pound note on the table, drank deeply, and returned to his conversation with Higgins.

"Do you have an address for Mr. Smith?"

"He said he was staying in Henley, but that weren't his real address. Mr. Smith was an American. No doubt about it. He was an American. He talked like a Yank. I'd guess he's from the south, but I wouldn't bet no money on it."

"How do you know he was staying at Henley-on-Themes?"

"He said he was. He was there about six weeks waitin' for his case. We had a number for him at a hotel in Henley. Don't have it no more. Threw it away as soon as he come for the case."

"Do you remember the name of the hotel?"

"No. As best I remember, my manager called anytime we needed to talk to Mr. Smith. I don't think I ever knew where he was staying."

"Six weeks seems like a long time to wait for a briefcase. Why so long?"

"I forgot to tell you the best part. Mr. Smith insisted on special leather. He wouldn't take no for an answer. It had to be a donkey hide. Don't ask me why. I had to send to Morocco for it—only place I could find a donkey hide. Took me three weeks to get it sent to London."

"Donkey hide? That is strange. I can't imagine why

it would make any difference. Is there something about donkey hide that makes it better than horsehide or cowhide?"

"Not that I know of, sir, and I've been doin' this for forty years. I'll never forget one thing, though. When he picked it up, he looked pleased, and told me how much he liked it. Then he said something real strange. He said it several times, he did. 'A jackass case for a jackass.'"

Joe surreptitiously took another hundred pound note out of his wallet and pushed it across the table. "Thanks for your help. If you can think of anything else, call me."

Joe finished his stout and then ordered another one. It was almost midnight when he left the Kings Arms. He walked back across the park to the Rubens and thought about his next move.

CHAPTER 16

Joe was up early the next day designing a business card on his laptop. He was soon finished and headed to a printer that advertised same day service. He left the card on a thumb drive at the printers and walked to Victoria Station where he made reservations for Henley the following day. The early train to Henley-on-Thames left out of Paddington Station. As he walked out of Victoria Station, rain began to pelt down upon his jacket.

They are sure right about this being a wet summer.

Joe ducked back into Victoria Station, found a kiosk doing a brisk business in cheap umbrellas, and availed himself of one. As he walked back to the Rubens for lunch, he considered his chances.

How can I find a man who stayed somewhere for only six weeks over twenty years ago? It may be impossible. I have been lucky so far to locate Higgins. What if he had retired? I'll bet no one else in that shop would remember the briefcase except Higgins. I don't even know where Mr. Smith stayed when he was in Henley or even what he looked like. The description I have could fit hundreds of people that have stayed in Henley for the last twenty years. Enough negative thinking. What do I have going for me?

Let's see. First, Henley is a rather small town and a tourist town. The shopkeepers probably know each other and have been living there forever. They just might remember someone who stayed in town for that long. Tourists are not memorable unless they are totally obnoxious or if they have a powerful personality. The ones that stay a few nights would be quickly forgotten. Someone staying for six weeks, even if he was bland, might be remembered. I'll bet a tall, handsome, younger, man would be remembered. He would probably have interacted with the locals if he was there that long. I can't believe anyone would stay in their room for six weeks. He would have talked to shopkeepers, bartenders,—somebody. They would, more than likely, have been permanent residents because tourists turn over too quickly to develop an ongoing acquaintance, much less a friendship. I think I have a chance of finding someone who will remember him, albeit a slim one.

When the train stopped in Henley the next morning, Joe stepped onto the platform and pulled up the handle of his roll-on suitcase. He tucked his umbrella under his arm, held the briefcase in his left hand, and headed up New Street looking for a hotel. New Street appeared to be anything but new. The half-timbered façades and weathered, red brick storefronts could have been here since the beginning of the Victorian era. About fifty yards from the river, Joe saw a large sign painted on the side of a building that said 'Henley Brewery' and housed inside was the Hotel du Vin.

Now, with a name like that, I bet a man could find something to drink there, he remarked to himself.

He pulled his suitcase inside and found the reception area. No one was at the desk so he rang the bell softly. Presently, a middle-aged woman came bustling down the hallway and greeted him warmly.

"Welcome to Henley," she said in a very British accent.

"We have rooms available. It's been a dreary summer, raining more than normal. How long will you be staying with us?"

"I will probably be here at least a week. Do you have a weekly rate?"

"I can give you a discount. Are you on business or holiday?"

"Business," replied Joe. "And I hope to have a little fun, also."

Joe showed his passport, the desk clerk made an imprint of his American Express card, and he was soon off to his room. The room was bright and cheerful with an internet connection and a modern television. The hotel brochure was prominently displayed on the desk and Joe quickly scanned the history of the building. As advertised, it had been a brewery before being renovated into a hotel. He unpacked, then took the stairs down to the ground floor and stepped out onto New Street. He strolled through the tourist section, noting the hotels, restaurants, and pubs where a visitor with six weeks to kill might frequent.

I wonder what this street looked like in 1989? he said to himself.

The Henley Regatta was in July, according to the rain-stained and sun-bleached posters that still hung from an occasional pole. Joe returned to his hotel by way of Hart Street which was lined with more of the same shops and tourist traps.

"This place could get old fast," he muttered.

He spent an hour in a corner pub eating a shepherd's pie and drinking a pint of Guinness, then headed back to his hotel.

"Are you all settled in, Mr. McPherson?" asked the desk

clerk as Joe entered the hotel. "Did you find everything you were looking for in town?"

Joe leaned casually against the counter and smiled at her engagingly. "Actually, the answer is no. I am looking for something in Henley, but it may be very difficult to find."

He extended his hand and said, "I am Joe McPherson. We haven't been formally introduced."

"I'm glad to meet you, Mr. McPherson. My name is Jenny Johnston."

"How long have you worked at the hotel, Jenny?"

"I have been here for about fifteen years now. I worked here part-time until my husband died in '99. I have been full-time since. I've lived in Henley my whole life."

"It's too bad about your husband, Jenny. He must have been quite young."

"He was only forty-four. Heart attack, it was. He just fell over one day and we took him to hospital. He died the next day."

"I'm very sorry to hear of your loss," remarked Joe. "And you never remarried?"

"Not too much chance of that here in Henley, Mr. McPherson. Not many eligible men around and them that are eligible are lookin' for some twenty year old."

"I think it's the same everywhere, Jenny."

"If you don't mind me askin', what kind of business brings you to Henley? There ain't that much goin' on around here except for selling trinkets and tending to the tourist trade."

Joe reached into his shirt pocket, got out one of his newly minted cards, and handed it to Jenny.

"That's me, J. P. McPherson, Private Investigator. That

is my cell phone number. No address. I don't stay in one place long enough to have one."

"So what do you investigate? I don't think we have much around here to investigate," said Jenny with a grin. "You might say it's pretty dull when you come right down to it."

"Can I level with you, Jenny? You seem like a very nice person and I think I can trust you. I don't usually discuss my cases with anyone, but I want to solve this one really badly."

"You have my word on it, Mr. McPherson," answered Jenny in a conspiratorial tone.

"Just call me Joe, please. I am working for a law firm that has offices in Washington, D.C. It is a very unusual case. I never had one anything like this before."

Jenny leaned over the desk and cocked her ear toward Joe as he continued.

"This law firm specializes in wills and trusts, mostly trusts for wealthy clients. This particular client is only nineteen years old. Her mother died about a year ago. The poor girl's mother had been an alcoholic for years. Her father has been dead since she was about ten. When her mother died, she left everything to—I'll call her Jane. Jane inherited quite a large sum. The interesting part is that her mother left a letter to be opened only after her death."

Joe looked both ways to see if anyone was in earshot and continued. Jenny leaned closer until her head was almost touching Joes.

"It seems Jane's mother had been an airline stewardess before she married. We call them flight attendants now. At any rate, she was flying from the West Coast to New York. This would have been in the early summer of 1989.

She met Mr. Smith on the flight. He was apparently traveling in First Class and she got to know him a little. When the plane landed at JFK, there was a weather delay, thunderstorms, or something."

Jenny looked up and saw Betty, her replacement, coming.

"Is it three o'clock already?" Jenny remarked, mainly to break off the conversation before Betty was within earshot. "How time flies."

"Could I buy you a pint and we could finish our conversation?" asked Joe.

"I'll buy you a pint just to hear the rest," Jenny responded in a whisper as Betty approached. "Meet me at the front door in five. I have to tally up the cash drawer before I leave. There's a nice quite pub just 'round the corner."

Joe ordered a Guinness and Jenny had a Newcastle Ale. They occupied a corner table in the Five Crowns and Jenny was anxious to hear the rest of the story.

"You know, it don't hurt my reputation none to be seen with a nice looking gentleman like yourself. Maybe some of the ol' losers around here will notice that I'm still alive. Now, go on and tell me what happened next with poor little Jane."

"Well, it seems Mr. Smith's plane was delayed and possibly canceled. That part is not clear, but what is clear is he and Jane's mother spent that night together. He flew out the next day and she went back to California. You can probably guess what happened next. Jane's mother found out she was pregnant. She knew it was Smith's, but she didn't want to contact him. She could hardly expect him to be responsible for a child since it had just been a one-night stand. All she knew about him was that he was heading to London and he had several bags with him. He told her he would be in England for one to two months."

"Mmmm…what did she do then, Joe?"

"She married an older man who had been pursuing her for a couple of years. They had apparently been dating off and on, and she told him she was pregnant with his baby. He married her and either didn't know or didn't care that Jane was not his. He had plenty of money. Jane's mother quit working and stayed home to raise her."

"And all those years Jane didn't know he wasn't her real father?" said Jenny looking and sounding forlorn. "How sad, yet he was a good father to her, I guess. If she didn't know, how could she feel anything but love for him?"

"Exactly," continued Joe. "Then, when her mother died and Jane read the letter her mother left her, she realized she might not be orphaned after all. She had a father out there she hadn't known existed and he had a beautiful daughter he didn't know about. And now, she had money enough to try to find him."

"Joe, this is just like a fairy tale in a story book."

I was thinking the same thing, thought Joe.

"In her mother's final letter," Joe continued, "she told Jane that Mr. Smith was traveling to England to attend the Henley Regatta. That is the last thing we know about him. I came here to try to pick up his trail and locate him."

"I want to help you find this Mr. Smith, Joe. I think I can help you. I know everyone in Henley and someone will remember him. I just know they will."

"There is a reward for finding him," said Joe. "I would like to see you get it."

"I don't want money for this, Joe. I want to do it for

Jane. I know what it's like to lose someone you love, and she never even knew her real father. How romantic."

"Believe me, Jenny. They won't miss the money. If you can help me, it would be greatly appreciated. We need to keep this quiet, though. I am not supposed to tell anyone or there could be a scandal."

"You can count on me, Joe. I will be discreet."

Right, Jenny, right, thought Joe.

CHAPTER 17

The next few days Joe walked around town and visited with the shopkeepers and innkeepers. He made a few discreet inquiries, but he left the heavy lifting to Jenny. Joe knew she was working because it was obvious people recognized him when he came into their establishments. His presence usually set off whispering, talking behind hands and the occasional giggle. He talked to Jenny when she was on duty and she kept him informed as to her progress. She had been in contact with the retired innkeepers and there were some who remembered someone who fit the description, but couldn't offer any additional information.

A week had passed since Joe had arrived in Henley. He was sitting in the bar of the Hotel du Vin when an older man walked across the room, pulled out a chair and sat down at his table.

"How about buyin' an ol' pensioner a drink?" he growled.

"I would be glad to have someone with whom to share a pint, my good man. Make yourself at home."

The pensioner motioned to the bartender who started drawing a Guinness. They sat in silence, sizing each other up, for the time it took to fill the pint glass with swirling brown liquid.

The bartender walked over with the overflowing glass on a tray, set it down on the table, and said, "Well, Willy, it looks like you've found someone to touch today."

"Never mind the sarcasm, Frank. You'll be paid and that's all you care about. Now leave us be. We have things to discuss."

Willy took a deep drink and then looked up at Joe from his perpetual slouch.

"I got some information you might be interested in, young feller. I hear you been asking about a Mr. Smith that stayed here back about twenty odd years ago."

"I might be interested in some information. However, you might as well know I am a very skeptical man. You aren't the first one to approach me about this. How will I know you are telling me the truth?"

"I ain't telling you nothin' lessen I get paid. I will tell you this. Smith was not his name."

"And what was his name?"

"And how much you payin?" said Willy as he drained his Guinness. "I'll have another, iffen you don't mind. I can feel myself loosening up about the tongue already."

Joe signaled the bartender for another drink and leaned closer to Willy. The stench of unwashed clothes repulsed him, but he persevered.

"If you have the information I need, I will pay you five hundred pounds. That is what it is worth to my client. You have to give me information I can verify. I will pay half down and half when I verify it."

"If that's the way you want to do it," replied Willy, "I'll tell you about half of what I know. Then, I'll tell you the other half when you pay me the rest of the money."

"Fair enough," responded Joe. "Now, where do we start?"

"I met this chap about twenty years ago. I had just retired and was drawin' me pension. I turned sixty that summer. This young fella, he was about thirty-five, I'd guess, came to Henley for the regatta. That's in July, you know, and he stayed on after everybody else left. I got to talking to him 'cause he would stand me to a pint or two."

"What did he look like?"

"He was tall and a good-looking man. Wore good clothes. I took him for a gentleman right away. He liked to drink a bit, but it never seemed to affect him much. He would get a little talkative sometimes, but he always walked straight and tall when he left."

"So far, you haven't told me anything I didn't know already. You're going to have to give me something new."

"I'll tell you something you don't know. His name was Henley, same as this town. He may have told everybody else that his name was Smith, but I know he was actually Oliver Henley, Dr. Oliver Henley."

"What kind of a doctor?"

"I don't know what kind of doctor he was, but he was a doctor of some kind. That's all you get for now. You give me my money and go do your verify or whatever. I'll be around when you are ready to hear the rest. Jenny knows where to find me."

Joe reached across the table and they shook hands. Willy felt the folded bills in Joe's hand and palmed them smoothly without changing his expression. Joe drained his glass, pushed back his chair, left the bar and mounted the stairs to his room. He looked at his phone and saw it was almost seven o'clock. It was still early in the States. Five hours time difference would make it about two in the afternoon.

What is today? Wednesday.

Joe opened the address book on his Treō and found the number for Ed Schultz.

I hope Ed will do this for me, he thought as he dialed the number on his new cell phone.

Ed answered on the second ring, "Schultz here. Can I help you?"

"Hi Ed. It's a voice out of the past," responded Joe. "How is everything at the old company?"

"Joe? Joe McPherson? How the hell are you? You sound good. Are you staying out of trouble these days?"

"Yes and no, Ed. I am calling you from England and I need something that only you can help me with. Listen, I know you can't talk now, but can I call you later after you get off work?"

"Sure. I'm curious now. I'll leave early today, about five o'clock, unless something really urgent comes up. Give me about thirty minutes to get home and call me there. Do you still have my home phone number?"

"Unless you've changed it. Thanks, Ed. I'll tell you about it later."

"I'm looking forward to talking to you Joe. See you then."

Joe fired up his computer and went online. He Googled Dr. Oliver Henley. No hits. He Googled Oliver Henley, without the doctor prefix.

Good, thought Joe. *A hit. Hmm, here is a Lord Henley, Oliver Michael Robert Eden 8th Baron of Henley. Served in the House of Lords. This doesn't sound like my man. No American Henleys popped up. Now, I wait until time to call Ed.*

Joe watched television and thought for the next three hours. *It seems unusual Henley didn't get any hits on Google.*

Most people had websites these days and if he was a medical doctor, he would probably have a practice. If he were a university professor, he would be publishing. I'll bet Willy is just stringing me along. I'll probably never see that guy again.

Joe's watch finally crept around to ten-thirty. He dialed Ed's number and Ed answered on the first ring.

"Hi Joe. Is that you? Your number came up 'unknown caller'. You must have a new phone number."

"Correct you are, Ed. I will give it to you later. I had to get one of those phones you can use anywhere in the world. As I told you, I am currently in England."

"What are you up to, Joe? It sounds like you have a new job. Can you tell me who you are working for these days?"

"I can't tell you now, Ed. I wish I could. I can tell you I am working for one of the most important men in the world. I know that sounds like BS, but in this case, it's absolutely true."

"I'm glad you are working again, Joe. You had me worried the last few years. You sound better than you have in a long time. How can I help you, Joe?"

"I am looking for someone that doesn't want to be found. I think he is responsible for committing a crime, and I need to locate him."

"Why don't you go to the police, Joe? That's what they do for a living, you know."

"Thanks a lot, Ed, for filling me in on that. If I could, I would have already been there. This is something I can't take to anyone just now. I need a favor."

"How can I help?"

"I think my man is a white male. He would be about fifty-five now. He possibly is a medical doctor or holds a doctorate in some branch of science, probably biology, or chemistry. He would have graduated in the 80's, probably from a good school. The name I have for him is Oliver Henley, H-e-n-l-e-y."

"Did you try Googling him?"

"It was the first thing I tried. No luck."

"No web site, no publications?"

"No. I couldn't find a trace of him. Ed, can you run him through the CIA computers and look for someone named Henley? Oliver is his given name, but possibly goes by initials only. I am assuming he graduated from a school in the United States in that time frame. I need to know if he exists and where I can find him."

"I think I can do that, Joe. I run ID's all day long and it shouldn't take long to see if he's in the database."

"Can I call you on your cell at lunch tomorrow? I don't want to call you at work anymore and they may be monitoring cell phones."

"Sure, Joe. I'll go out to lunch tomorrow. Call me about 12:15 Eastern. I should have something for you by then."

"Thanks, Ed. I will owe you a big one."

"No problem, Joe. I'm just glad to hear from you and everything is all right. Let's get together when you get back to D.C."

"Sounds good, Ed. Call you tomorrow. Have a good evening. Goodbye."

Joe turned off the light and went to sleep thinking about Dr. Oliver Henley.

CHAPTER 18

It was nearing five o'clock in England and Joe was imagining Ed should just be leaving work to have lunch. Waiting for the time to pass was excruciating. Joe remembered an old Tom Petty song, 'Waiting is the Hardest Part' and he thought about how long it was until Christmas finally came when he was a kid.

Maybe patience is a virtue, thought Joe, *but it is possibly the least of the virtues.*

Joe had walked the streets of Henley all day without good reason. It was easier to walk than to wait in his room. He thought about going back to the Five Crowns, but he knew he needed to be stone cold sober when he talked to Ed. It had drizzled all day. One of those days when you really didn't need an umbrella or rain coat, but the drizzle just hung in the air and everything felt damp and clammy. His clothes were neither wet nor dry, just soggy and limp like a stale soda cracker. He talked to Jenny and she had lots to report, but nothing that was worth following up on. Even the tourists were subdued. He saw an attractive woman just about noon, but she disappeared into a shop before he could strike up a conversation. It was funny, now that he had cut back on drinking; he was attracted to women again.

No hard liquor for over three weeks now. Not bad, he thought. Finally, it was time to call Ed. Joe was relieved when Ed answered on the first ring.

"Hi Joe. I have your number in my phone now," answered Ed.

"What did you find out?"

"I think I have your man, Joe. There were several Henley's that received doctorates, but the one I think you're looking for is a Dr. Howard O. Henley. The O is for Oliver. I assume he goes by Oliver or Ollie as opposed to Howie or Howard. Remember Ollie North? Anyway, he graduated from Scripps Institute in 1985. His degree was in Molecular Biology."

"Sounds promising. Scripps is a good school. I thought about going there. La Jolla weather is a hell of a lot better than D.C.—not to mention I wouldn't have met Kim. What else do we know about Dr. Henley?"

"First, you are right about not publishing anything. Except for his Ph.D. thesis, he hasn't had a single publication. I can't find any record of him going to work anywhere. Here is the most interesting part. He hasn't filed income tax returns since he left graduate school. He was on a fellowship at Scripps, but after he left, he seems to have dropped out of sight. As an aside, his grandparents immigrated from England. Odds are the family name derives from Henley-on-Thames."

"That has to be him, Ed. He sounds like my man. Maybe the guy you found just died or something. Do you have an address?"

"He isn't dead or I would have found his obit. His last known address is a rural route near Louisville, Kentucky. I can text you his social and the mailing address. Is there anything else I can do to help?

"Not now, Ed. I definitely owe you one. I can't thank you enough."

"No problem, Joe. It was great hearing from you. Don't wait so long next time. I'm sure glad you're feeling better. Keep it up, Joe."

Joe took the stairs down to the ground floor and went into the bar. Jenny had been gone since three. He did not know how to contact her on off hours, so he approached the bartender.

"Have you seen Willy today?" asked Joe.

"He came in earlier this afternoon, but left about an hour ago. He usually hangs out at the Five Crowns when he has money and he seems to have come into some lately. He's even buying a pint or two for his drinkin' buddies."

"Thanks," said Joe as he turned to leave. *That's a good sign*, thought Joe. *He was probably waiting for me to come down. If he was lying, he would have skipped.*

Willy was sitting at a corner table in the Five Crowns with another man who was equally disheveled when Joe entered the bar. Willy motioned for his companion to leave and invited Joe over.

"Have you got your verification yet?" asked Willy with a definite slur in his voice.

"Maybe," Joe responded as he sat down. The bartender was watching to see if Joe was ordering and Joe nodded affirmatively. "I might be willing to buy some more information if you have any to sell."

"Let me see the color of your money first, mate. Then we can talk. I have plenty more to tell you."

Joe put a hundred pound note on the table. Willy reached for it and Joe pulled it back.

"Let's have a little trust here, Willy. I am an honest man and I have already paid you more than you get in a month. I'm not going anywhere until I get my information."

Willy sat back, picked up his glass, and took a draught of Guinness. Then he hunched over the table and started talking.

"I met Oliver Henley in July of '89. I got to know him pretty well, as much as he would let anyone know him I'll be willing to speculate. He was a brilliant man. He brought a book with him every time he went anywhere, even to the pub. He'd sit and read them thick books for hours. Sometimes he'd talk to me about horses. He was a horse man. He knew more about horses than anyone I ever knew."

"Give me an example," interrupted Joe. "How do you know he knew horses?"

"There used to be a betting bar at the end of New Street. They had satellite TV and you could watch the horse races from everywhere in the world. You could bet on the ponies. Your Mr. Smith used to invite me along sometimes. I'll tell you, that man could look at the horses comin'out of the paddock walking to the starting gates and he could pick the winner almost every time. He'd say, 'Look at the hindquarters on that one, Willy, and the small head. He's got some Arabian in him. He'll start slow, but he'll come on at the end and win'. Or, sometimes he'd say, 'Look at the way that one moves sideways. He's the most athletic horse in the field. He'll find a way to win'. And, sure enough, that horse would come up on the rail and it'd look like he was hemmed in, but he'd break out somehow and jump up on the lead."

"Did he bet on the horses?"

"I never knew of him to bet, not once. With him, it was just like he was studying them. It was like he was trying to understand what made the difference between a winner and a loser."

"How do you know his name is Oliver Henley?"

"That's an easy one. Everybody that drinks has to go to the men's room. I looked at his books while he was gone. He had his name in them. I have to remember Henley. How could I forget that! And Oliver. Oliver Twist. Dickens, you know. Every schoolboy in England has to read about ol' Oliver Twist."

"What kind of books did he read?"

"His books were thick textbooks, some kind of science books. He used to go over to the University at Oxford two or three times a week and go to the library. It's only about forty kilometers to Oxford and the train goes there and back every day. I think he knew some of the teachers there. Dons, they call 'em."

"That makes sense. He spent time reading here and he could collaborate with colleagues at Oxford," Joe reasoned. "A nice way to spend the summer."

"If you say so, Joe. I don't know about collaborate, but he went there a lot."

"Is there anything else you can remember, Willy? Anything you haven't told me?"

"I can't think of anything else. You're gonna' try to cheat me out of the rest of my money, ain't you?" said Willy contentiously.

Joe took out the rest of the money and handed it discreetly to Willy.

"You have been very helpful. I am glad we met. I hope you spend this wisely."

"Don't worry, Joe. I will," said Willy with a wide grin

that revealed more blank spaces than teeth. "Every penny will be spent on the best drinks Henley has to offer."

Joe went back to his room, got on the internet, and started making reservations. He found a British Airways flight out of Heathrow that connected through JFK to Louisville. The plane didn't leave until five o'clock tomorrow. *That should leave plenty of time to get to London on the train and check in.*

He made the reservation and decided to go back to the bar for a couple of drinks.

Joe returned to his room shortly before eleven. He opened his suitcase and started cleaning everything out of the bureau drawers. It always seemed like there was more to pack every time he made a stop.

It's human nature to collect stuff, he reflected. *No matter how hard I try to keep it simple, I keep accumulating things. Where can I pack the umbrella? Maybe it will rain tomorrow and I'll need it.*

Joe sat down at the desk and started shutting down his computer. *I would have sworn I put this thing to sleep.* Joe closed the British Airways web site and shut down. He packed the briefcase with everything that wouldn't fit in the carry-on and hit the bed. He slept soundly for the first time in the last two weeks.

Joe was down in the lobby to check out by seven the next morning and was relieved to find Jenny already at work.

"I'm sure glad to see you today. I am checking out and I owe you something."

Joe opened his wallet, counted out twenty hundred-pound notes, and handed them to Jenny.

"Joe. I couldn't possibly take this. I didn't find your man yet. Anyway, this is too much. I can't."

"Trust me, Jenny. You found my man for me. I promised I wouldn't tell anyone where I got the information, but I found Mr. Smith because of you. I couldn't have done it without you. You deserve this and you can use it, I'm sure."

"If you get poor little Jane and her real father together, that will be reward enough."

"Believe me, Jenny, they won't even miss the money, I guarantee it. You have done a good thing. Take the money and enjoy it."

"I'm going to miss you, Joe. Will I ever see you again?"

"I hope so, Jenny. Thanks again for your help. I will take one of your hotel post cards," said Joe as he put a card in his pocket. "I will try to drop you a line if and when I find Mr. Smith."

"Good bye, Joe. Give me a hug."

CHAPTER 19

The sun was out and the verdant fields of central England glistened with raindrops left over from the night before. The train stopped at every small town along the way to London, but Joe was in no hurry. He had the entire day to catch his plane and he was enjoying the ride. The morning train slowly emptied as passengers, already mentally engaged in the coming day's work, scurried toward their offices and shops every time the car doors opened.

Eventually, Joe found himself almost alone and he decided to call Cardinal O'Riley. *The international cell phone was a great invention. I can call anywhere in the world from a moving train in England. Just in my lifetime, the ability to communicate has made a quantum leap.* Joe pressed the speed dial for the cardinal's cell phone.

"Hello, Joe," answered Cardinal O'Riley. "I haven't heard from you for almost a week. How is it going? Have you made any progress?"

"I think I have found our man, Cardinal. It's a long story and I want to tell it all to you some day, but the short version is that the mysterious Mr. Chevalier is actually Dr. Oliver Henley."

"Have you actually seen him?" responded the cardinal excitedly.

"No. As far as I can determine, he hasn't been back here since just before he took the relics."

"Where is here, Joe?" asked the cardinal.

"Henley, England," said Joe. "He stayed here about a month back in the summer of 1989."

"The same as Henley-on-Thames?"

"The very same. I don't know if there is a connection yet. In any case, I have an address, a bit old, but his last known is just outside Louisville, Kentucky. I have reservations on a plane out of Heathrow at five this afternoon for JFK. I'll be in Louisville tomorrow."

"That's fantastic, Joe. Are you sure this is our man? How did you find him after all these years?"

"I'm pretty sure this is the right guy, Cardinal. He has a Ph.D. in molecular biology and he fits the description I have of him. I'll tell you how later when we have a couple of hours."

"Joe, I think you are getting close, dangerously close. These men are ruthless. If we are correct, they have been planning to do something like this for centuries. Most of us don't can't think in terms of centuries, Joe. They have been plotting this vendetta for many years, passing the hate down from generation to generation. They will do whatever it takes. The closer you get to this man and his organization, the more likely you are to be eliminated. Remember, if they are determined to bring down the Church, they will certainly not hesitate to kill if someone gets in their way."

"Thanks for the advice, Cardinal. I will be careful. So far, I don't think anyone even knows I am looking for them. As long as I can remain anonymous, I am safe. My plan is to find this elusive Dr. Henley and confirm he is responsible for the theft. Then we will have to bring in the authorities. We can't take the law into our own hands."

"Joe, we can't let this information get out to the

public. We must handle it internally. When you find Dr. Henley, you call me. I will take it from there. Do you understand?"

"I hear you, Cardinal. I'm going to ring off now. We are coming into Paddington Station and I have to gather up my belongings. I'll call you when I get more information."

CHAPTER 20

Cardinal O'Riley looked at the cell phone for a few seconds after the call light dimmed. He sat back in his leather executive chair and stared straight ahead, thinking for a few moments. He made his decision and reached for a small, leather bound book he kept in his inside pocket and dialed.

"Sean, is that you? This is Father O'Riley. Yes, you can call me Cardinal if you like. Sean, I have a great favor to ask of you. You know I always helped you when we were fighting the British in Belfast. Thank you, Sean. Yes, we did raise a lot of money for the IRA back in those days. Sean, I have a situation that could threaten the very foundations of the Church. Yes, I am serious and no, I am not exaggerating. I need you to go to Louisville, Kentucky, and wait for me to call. I have a man that will arrive there tomorrow. His name is Dr. Joseph McPherson. I don't know where he will be staying. Do not make contact with him. I need you to keep an eye on him. He may be in danger and it would be better if he didn't know you were there. I am also concerned if it gets rough, he won't have the guts to finish the job."

"Sean, I'll level with you. This could get ugly. Do you have a gun? You had better bring it. You're right. It's better to drive. How long does it take from New York? A couple of days is probably all right. It'll take Joe that long to find this man, if he is still there. Take whatever time you need today to get your business in order and then get down to Louisville. A rental would be best. Do you need any money, Sean? I'll arrange for you to pick up a credit card today. Bless you, Sean Hanratty. May God go with you."

CHAPTER 21

"Would you care for a glass of champagne, Dr. McPherson," said the flight attendant in a crisp English accent as she stood over Joe. "We have been delayed for a few minutes at the gate. I'm very sorry for the inconvenience."

"I don't mind. I have a two hour layover at JFK. I will take you up on that drink."

When she returned she put the plastic glass of champagne on the arm of Joe's seat and said in a low voice, "Dr. McPherson, we have a few seats left in First Class. I know from the manifest you paid full fare for Business. Would you like to move up to First?"

"I don't mind of I do. I have never sat in First Class. To be honest, I bought my ticket at the last minute and they didn't have anything left in Coach."

"Do you have luggage in the overhead?" inquired the flight attendant.

Joe grabbed his carry-on and followed the pretty, young attendant to First Class. She stowed his luggage and went forward to the kitchen area. She soon returned with a silver plate of smoked salmon and brie and a crystal glass of champagne. She smiled pleasantly as she served him and then brought him a pillow, blanket, and a small leather pouch that contained a toothbrush, foot warmers, and other travel incidentals. Joe reclined his seat and savored the experience. He was almost disappointed when the Airbus taxied to the runway and departed.

When the pilot turned off the seatbelt light, the flight attendant returned and asked Joe if he cared for a drink. Joe hesitated and then decided.

"Have you any Absolut vodka?"

"Of course," she responded. "I have Beluga caviar also. They go well together. Would you care for some?"

The flight attendant brought a sumptuous plate of caviar and toast points, and a shot glass of vodka. Joe took the miniature butter knife and spread the black fish roe on the toast, savored it, and then chased it down with the vodka. He looked around the cabin and observed the First Class passengers as they enjoyed the luxury of being served the finest foods as the aircraft hurtled toward their destination in the United States. Joe looked out of the window to his left and saw Ireland pass beneath him, getting smaller as they gained altitude. The aircraft leveled off at 38,000 feet and the powerful turbine engines were humming with a comforting low frequency vibration that he felt more than heard. The sound of the thin air rushing by the fuselage provided a reassuring background sound imbued a sense of speed and purpose. The vodka warmed his stomach and relaxed him. The warmth seeped through his body, up along his spinal column, and soon reached his brain. The anxieties of the past weeks were overwhelmed by growing euphoria, a sensation that he was completely surrounded by pleasure and comfort.

Joe found the button that reclined his seat. He opened his eyes and the pretty, smiling flight attendant was filling his shot glass.

Absolute is smooth, he reflected. *How could I keep drinking that rotgut Popov?*

Joe took note of the other First Class passengers.

They were wearing Rolex watches, Prada dresses, Christian Louboutin shoes. They were at ease with their surroundings. This was not their first time in First Class, for sure. They expected this treatment. This was their life style. No wonder Cardinal Stancampiano was vulnerable to a bribe. Being spoiled was definitely habit forming.

Joe leaned over and looked out of the window at the blue expanse of ocean stretching to the horizon. There were a few scattered clouds hovering just above the water that added perspective to the cerulean seascape below.

The temperature at this altitude is sixty degrees below zero, he remembered. *Winter or summer, the temperature doesn't change that much. The pressure outside is only about four pounds per square inch. They only pressurize the cabin to ten thousand feet or about ten pounds per square inch. No wonder this vodka is so potent. I am oxygen deficient and the alcohol blocks the receptors in my brain. God, I loved to learn about science. I couldn't wait to be a real scientist. Now I know all these things and a lot more and I am wasting my life and not using my education. I wonder if I could go back to work? Would someone give me another chance?*

"Would you care for dinner, Dr. McPherson?" asked the lovely flight attendant, interrupting Joe's introspection.

"I apologize," responded Joe. "I haven't even looked at the menu. Can you give me a minute?"

"Take all the time you need, Dr. We have a long flight ahead. I will bring you more caviar. I'll be right back."

Joe decided on the braised beef tips and while he waited, he sipped another Absolut. The dinner was excellent. He chose a French Bordeaux to go with his meal and Grand Marnier for dessert.

Joe McPherson couldn't resist reflecting on how

different his life could have unfolded if he hadn't met Kim. He was happy working in the laboratory and teaching. Academia had insulated him from the real world. Of course, there was the struggle to get tenure and gain a reputation in his field, but Joe had never been in science for the money or prestige. If you really loved your work, that was reward enough. Being paid for what you would do free was the best life had to offer. Pressure came from trying to live up to someone else's expectations. The secrets of nature were often difficult to unravel, but they were at least logical. With patience and cunning, they were tractable. Science was like solving a very complex puzzle where you discover clues by hard work and eventually they led you to the right answer. He understood the rational world. Kim represented the irrational world that befuddled him. When done correctly, science was infinitely reproducible. In Kim's world, identical stimuli never produced the same result. It depended on her mood at the time.

Joe felt the nose of the plane tilt slightly down and the engines throttle back. They were starting the long decent into JFK. It would still be an hour until the final approach, but the end had begun. Joe felt a tinge of regret.

When the First Class door opened, the passengers, queued up in the aisles, marched stoically out of the plane, and up the gangway toward customs. He caught a glimpse of the night sky as he entered the jet way and tried to remember what time it was in New York. He decided it didn't matter since they were presumably on time and he would catch his connecting flight to Louisville. He trudged to the customs line, awaited his turn to produce a passport, and exited the gate into the terminal. He consulted a monitor in the terminal, determined his next leg was on time, and then headed for the gate.

I have an hour to kill, he decided and walked into the bar next to his gate. *I liked that Absolut so well, I think I will try a Grey Goose,* he thought.

Two drinks later, he boarded the plane to Louisville and fell asleep. The next thing he remembered was landing in Kentucky.

CHAPTER 22

The GPS unit in the rental came in handy and Joe soon arrived at the Hilton Inn and Suites. The night desk clerk efficiently processed his America Express and handed him the plastic rectangle that gave him access to his room.

"Do you have a restaurant?" Joe inquired.

"The Winners Circle Lounge is open until two. They have a limited selection of food, sir. Our main restaurant is closed."

Joe dropped off his luggage in the room, returned to the lobby, and found the Winners Circle. He settled into a red leatherette booth and picked up the plastic covered menu.

A tall thin, hard looking waitress wearing a name tag that read 'Terri' soon appeared at his table and in a bored voice asked, "What's yours, buddy?"

"Let's start out with a martini, Terri. I'll take a look at the menu while you're getting my drink," Joe replied.

"Don't wait too long. The kitchen closes in thirty minutes," said Terri as she sauntered back behind the bar.

She returned with his drink and Joe ordered a club sandwich. He sipped his martini and began to think about tomorrow. He had an address for Dr. Henley, but he sincerely doubted the GPS unit would know how to find a rural route. *Maybe I can go to the post office and get the routes from them.* The martini began to restore his euphoria and he decided to worry about getting there tomorrow. Joe looked at his watch. It was almost eight a.m. in England. *This had been a long day.*

When the sandwich came, he ordered another martini. Terri brought him a double.

"Compliments of the house," she announced as she set it down.

Joe finished about half of his sandwich and all the contents of the martini glass. He finally decided it was time to go to bed. He waived to Terri for the check and signed it to his room. He was a little wobbly as he arose from the table, but he found his feet soon enough and headed for the elevator. The elevator was painfully slow in arriving. Finally the door opened. Joe entered and pushed the button for the seventh floor. The elevator lurched upward. He needed to go to the bathroom badly, he decided. *Elevators always do that to me*, Joe mused as the door opened and staggered out to find room 714.

Joe stood at the entry to the long hallways and tried to determine from the numbers on the wall which corridor led to his room. Finally, he decided he was between rooms 700 and 750 and shambled down that hallway. As he approached the room, he fumbled through his pants pocket for the plastic card. *I hope this thing works. I can't hold it if I have to go back the front desk for a new card.*

Joe slipped the plastic card into the electronic keyway slot and removed it quickly. He saw the light turn green and heard the familiar click of the lock opening. He opened the door and started for the bathroom when he was pushed inside and thrown to the floor.

As Joe fell forward into his room, he was struck from behind by something heavy. He fell limply to the floor and passed out from a combination of alcohol and the impact on his head. As he fought to regain consciousness, he could hear a woman's authoritative voice, apparently speaking into the phone.

"Hello Terri. Your friend is in the hallway outside of 714. Send someone to drag him out of the building or I will call the manager. Oh, I'm sure you don't know anything about it. If he isn't gone in thirty minutes, I'm calling the front desk."

The last thing Joe remembered was the sound of the telephone handset slam into its cradle.

CHAPTER 23

Joe began to wake slowly, trying to remember where he was. The pale morning light was sneaking past the edges of the blackout drapes filling the room with dark, hazy shadows. His head was pounding to the rhythm of his heart. Joe ran his hand over the back of his head and found a very sensitive prominent lump he didn't remember and a sticky substance that felt like partially dried blood.

Why am I on the floor? he asked himself as he raised up on his elbow and began to assess his situation. *Vodka doesn't usually fight back.*

After a visit to the bathroom, Joe headed for the bed. Just as he reached to turn back the covers, he was startled by the sound of a woman's voice.

"Not here, mister. Try the couch. We'll talk tomorrow. Now, get some sleep and try to get through that hangover. You must have a beauty this morning. Goodnight."

The next time Joe awoke, he heard the sound of the shower. A female voice was humming an unfamiliar song.

That must be the person in my bed last night, Joe thought. *I sure wish I felt like singing in the shower. I must be getting out of drinking condition. Not enough practice lately, I guess.*

Joe pulled the blanket over his head and curled up on the couch.

He heard the bathroom door open and then someone pulled the blanket back. Standing over him was a very attractive, athletic looking woman looking down at him with an enigmatic smile. She continued to towel her dark, curly hair as she addressed Joe.

"Are you planning to sleep all day? We have things to do, Joe. Get a shower and I'll order a pot of coffee."

She opened her purse, took out a sealed metal vial, unscrewed the lid, and shook out a small white tablet.

"Take this. You'll feel better by the time you get out of the shower. Throw those clothes out to me. I'll send them to the laundry. You stink. God, what a mess!"

Joe started to protest, but didn't. He knew when he was bested. He went to the bathroom, undressed, and tossed out the clothing he had worn for several days. She was right about the tablet. He was singing by the time he was finished showering.

When Joe returned to the room, his visitor was sitting on the couch. Her black hair had dried and arranged itself into a natural cap of curls. She was dressed in black slacks and a dark grey knit top. She wore little makeup. She poured Joe a cup of coffee.

"You like it black with sweetener, right? You prefer the pink kind, but the blue will do in a pinch. It is nice to meet you, Joe McPherson."

"I am please to meet you, too, Miss?"

"Call me Myra. I think we can start out on a first name basis."

"Would you please tell me what you are doing in my room, Myra?" said Joe as he sipped his coffee.

"Trying to keep you alive, Joe. I have too much invested in you to let you die on me now."

"What happened last night? The last thing I remember is opening the door. Then I went blank."

"You were actually pretty lucky. The waitress in the lounge, remember Terri? She set you up. She knew you were out of control and called her sleazy boyfriend. When you got to your room, he was waiting for you in the hall. I think they were going to roll you and leave you in the room. When you woke up, you wouldn't know what hit you and you probably wouldn't report it anyway. I suspect it happens regularly here in the hotel."

"Where were you? I don't remember seeing you last night?"

"I was sitting in the corner, watching. Terri pegged you as a mark from the minute you walked in the door. Joe, you are a smart man, but in my world you are as helpless as a kitten."

"How do you know me? I have never seen you before in my life."

Myra smiled. "What about the girl in St. James Park? If I remember, you said something like, 'nice butt'."

"I remember seeing a runner. How do you know what I said? I just thought it."

"You have a habit of mumbling out loud when you're thinking. Lots of people do it subconsciously."

"How did you hear me? What the hell is going on!"

"I'm going to level with you, Joe. I am not supposed to do this, but you are a nice man. I know you better than you realize because I know the real Joe. The one that exists when no one is around."

"And how do you know?"

"I have been following you since you left the Vatican. I watched you buy the computer and cell phone. I put a parasitic transponder in your phone. It draws off your battery and transmits your conversations on a gap FM frequency. I can pick up the signal for about a mile with my receiver. It looks like a Sony Walkman, but it has a lot of extra features. The first time you left your room in Henley, I put a program on your laptop so I can network on Bluetooth. I can operate your computer remotely if I need to. That's how I downloaded your plane reservations."

"How did you get into my room?" asked Joe.

"That's easy. We have electronic keys that automatically cycle through all possible combinations on the magnetic lock. It works better than the hotel key."

"Who are you? Who do you work for?"

"That I can't tell you. But I can tell you we are on the same side."

"How much do you know about what I'm doing?"

"I know you are looking for a mysterious Dr. Henley, Oliver Henley. He apparently has stolen something from the Vatican that they want back very badly. Whatever this thing is, they are afraid it could bring down the Catholic Church, as we know it. I think it is some type of historical evidence or belongings of Jesus Christ. Whatever it is, it might prove if Jesus is who he claimed to be. If that is true, my organization is also very interested in finding it. One thing I do know, Joe, you are in danger and the closer you get to finding Dr. Henley, the greater the danger."

"Why can't you tell me who you work for?"

"Let's just say we were here before the Christians. Now that we are working together, what can you tell me I don't already know?"

"I will confide in you, Myra. I know I need help. I am not the right guy for this assignment. I worked for the CIA, but I never left the laboratory once in twenty years. I was an analyst. I analyzed the bits and pieces the field agents would bring back. I'd tell them what they might mean, if certain things were possible, and how they might be used as weapons or to cause mischief. I was trained as a molecular biologist. Biology is my world, not this secret agent stuff."

"I have to tell you, I was impressed by the way you found Oliver Henley. Your story about poor little Jane was a real tearjerker. You also found the right person to help you. Jenny Johnston is connected in Henley. She knows everyone there. That was a stroke of genius."

"Just luck, I suppose. I hope I didn't use her wrongly."

"Joe, you made her a hero and raised her self esteem. The money you gave her was very generous. That is when I knew I liked you. You are a good man. You have your foibles, but basically, you're a good man."

"Thanks, Myra. And I want to thank you for saving my bacon last night. You're right. I was as helpless as a kitten. How stupid can I be?"

"Let's move on. Now tell me everything you know about this Henley character. What did he steal? Why is the Church so concerned?"

"Order another pot of coffee. This may take a while. Did you ever hear of the Knights Templar?"

"Hold on, Joe. I have a better idea. Why don't you order lunch and a pot of coffee from room service? I am going to check out of my room. If I'm going to keep the bad guys at bay, I might as well be here. You get the couch. OK? I'll be right back with my stuff. See if they are still serving breakfast. Get me an omelet, egg whites, veggies, and whole wheat. No ham, bacon, or sausage, and no butter."

"Coming right up, madam," said Joe with an impish grin.

CHAPTER 24

Joe drove his rented Ford Torus out to the 264 loop and took the Mount Washington exit. He continued toward Bardstown and soon found himself in horse country. Whitewashed wooden fences lined the road and the Kentucky bluegrass was almost waist high in the fields waiting for the upcoming haying season. It had been a rainy summer and the grass lived up to its name. Thoroughbred horses populated the fields. Some were running just for the pure enjoyment of it. The morning sunlight reflected off their sleek coats as their muscles contracted. They glided effortlessly over the verdant fields. Their hooves seemed to contact the earth much too infrequently as if defying gravity.

Myra was following about two miles back. They had decided to take both cars. Joe would approach the farm and inquire about Dr. Henley. Myra would listen on her Walkman. She had gotten the lat-long location of the farm from her source, whoever that was, and they had Googled the coordinates. The farm appeared to be situated on a half section of well-developed land. Several barns were visible in the satellite photo and the main house appeared to have a footprint of approximately four thousand square feet. The driveway was about a quarter mile long and terminated at the house. Myra planned to approach the house from the north side. A dense copse of trees provided cover and her transponder would pick up signals from Joe's cell phone.

Joe turned into the driveway. His tires rumbled across the pipes that formed the cattle guard and crunched on the gravel driveway, as he drove slowly between the white rail fences. As he approached the rambling one-story house, he saw the screen door open and a man walk out onto the front porch. The man watched intently as Joe parked the Torus and got out.

"Hello," said Joe. "I am looking for Dr. Oliver Henley. Is this his farm?"

The khaki-clad man walked slowly down the steps and approached Joe without responding. When he came within proximity, Joe extended his hand.

"I'm Joe McPherson. I went to school with Oliver. Is he home?"

"No one by that name lives here, mister," said the man ignoring Joe's outstretched hand. "You must have the wrong address."

"I was sure this is the right farm. Have you lived here long, Mr. …?"

"Name's Carl. I've lived here for a long time, Mr. McPherson, and I never heard of anyone named Henley. Now, if you don't mind, I've got work to do. I think you can find your way out."

"I'm sorry to have bothered you," responded Joe getting back into his car. "I will check the address again. I must have made a mistake."

The man returned to the porch and watched as Joe pulled around the circular drive and headed the car back toward the highway. Just as Joe turned onto the hard surface road, his cell phone rang.

"There is a truck stop back on 264," said Myra. "I'll meet you there."

Joe pulled into the parking lot of the truck stop. He parked next to the diner, entered, and found a booth. Myra followed him into the restaurant shortly, slid gracefully into the booth, and ordered a cup of coffee.

"The guy is lying, of course," said Myra in a low voice as soon as the server was out of earshot. "I talked to headquarters this morning and they have proof of mail coming to Henley at that address up until about five years ago. He didn't file a change of address, but the mail gradually stopped. We know he lived there. The person you talked to was either Carl Brundidge or Paul Warner. Both names are probably assumed. They are the only people who get mail at that address except letters addressed to 'current resident'. Did you get a chance to see anything that might be unusual?"

"Actually, I guess I didn't think about it. The man I talked to said his name was Carl. At least that checks with your information. I didn't see anything unusual or otherwise. I was too busy trying to deal with Carl."

"A fine secret agent you make."

"What should I have been looking for?"

"That's the whole point, Joe. We don't know exactly what we are looking for, so we look for anything out of the ordinary. Anything that does not look like it belongs at a horse farm. That is what we're looking for."

"Oh. Why didn't you tell me?"

"You're the one with the Ph.D. I thought it would be obvious."

"What do we do now, Sherlock?"

"We go back. We tried the frontal approach, now we try the back door. Get in your car and follow me. We need to get you some dark clothes and black athletic shoes. We will come back tonight. There is a moon, but it doesn't rise until later. We should be all right around midnight. Let's move it. We have work to do."

Myra opened the door to room 714 and held it for Joe as he guided several large Wal-Mart shopping bags through the opening.

"Put them down on the bed, Joe. We have work to do before tonight."

"I'll be interested in seeing what you have in mind for some of these things."

Myra began to sort out the purchases.

"These are for tonight. The black jogging suit will keep you warm and doesn't restrict movement. The nylon material is partially water resistant and doesn't catch on bushes and briars as much as cotton or wool. The black ski mask won't reflect light from your head and face. Keep it pulled down when we get close to the house and barns. Here is your flashlight. Take the black electricians tape and cover the lens except for a slit about ten millimeters wide. That's enough light to see what you need to see. Wear the black socks with the sneakers."

"What do you intend to do with the pellet pistol? Do you plan to try to pretend it is a real weapon?"

"When I get though with it, it will be lethal enough. Since we can't purchase a gun without waiting several days for the permit, it will have to do. I got the repeater. This gun holds about twenty BB's. The gas cylinder will last through several reloads. That will be more than enough."

"I don't think you will stop anyone with BB's, Myra. You might just make them angrier."

"Grab that bag and follow me. We are going to make a little ammo. Open the rubber gloves and put on a pair.

Here, hold these tweezers. These damn plastic packages are frustrating. Hand me the knife. I like this hunting knife. It has a good feel to it."

Myra opened her suitcase and took out a cosmetic bag. She opened it and retrieved a small vial of nail polish.

"The color is nice, don't you think? It's called Chinese Red. Stand back, Joe."

Myra slipped on the rubber gloves and cautiously opened the nail polish.

"Pick up one of the BB's with the tweezers. That's good. Hold it over the lavatory."

Myra carefully painted the BB Chinese Red and then picked up the hotel hair dryer. She dried the BB and indicated for Joe to place it in her gloved hand.

"Do you know what curare is, Joe?"

"I know it is used by natives along the Amazon. They put it on the tips of their blowgun darts. I think it is made from a plant that is indigenous to the region."

"Very good. This is what I call Super Curare. It is similar to the original, but much stronger. It attacks the nervous system. I shoot for the eyes. The pain is excruciating and totally debilitating. The poison attacks the ocular nerves and spreads to the brain, shutting down the heart and respiratory system. It takes less than ten seconds. The pellet will penetrate unprotected skin. It takes longer to kill if you miss the eyes, but it is still effective. We will make enough for tonight and load the gun. I don't think we will need it, but I want to be prepared. This nail polish is also a sure cure for impulsive nail biting, so be careful. Now, if you will finish making these little babies, I will go down and work on the car. I need to disable the interior lights and all the warning buzzers. No use announcing our presence."

CHAPTER 25

It was almost midnight when they drove slowly past the long driveway leading to the farmhouse. Myra had cut the lights two miles back and was driving by watching the berm. She had rolled down her window so she didn't have to look through the slightly tinted glass.

"I don't see any lights," she said in a low voice. "I think they have turned in for the night. It's good and dark, a perfect night for reconnaissance."

"How can you see in the dark?" asked Joe. "I can't see anything."

"I've had radial keratotomy on both eyes. It is one of the perks of my job. I have 20/10 vision. That is the same as Chuck Yeager and Ted Williams, except theirs was natural. Never underestimate the ability to see better than everyone else."

"I'm beginning to feel very inferior," said Joe. "My self esteem wasn't that good to begin with."

"You are a brilliant man, Joe. Don't ever forget that. Now, remember what I told you. These things can keep you alive. First, we probably won't have any contact with these people. We are looking for information, not confrontation. You go to the outlying barns and see what you can find. I will take the house. We must assume they are sleeping there, but we can't be one-hundred percent sure. If I call your cell phone, it will vibrate, right?"

"Right."

"Do not answer it. The phone lights up and makes you a target. Keep it in the waistband pocket in your running pants. You can feel it vibrating better and it is harder to find if you are caught. I will let the phone ring once if you need to get the hell out. If it rings twice, meet me at the first barn. If it rings three times, hide and try to get back to the car when you can. Got it?"

"Got it."

"When we get on the premises, stay alert. Your first priority is to be aware of your surroundings. For every minute you spend looking for something, spend two minutes looking for someone that could compromise you. Do not become complacent. Watch for the enemy. Got it?"

"Got it."

Myra guided the car onto the berm through the shallow ditch and parked in a stand of trees about one hundred meters from the road. They opened the doors and put on their small, black backpacks.

"Joe," she whispered, "when you close the door, just push it until it latches."

"Got it."

"Follow me and walk slowly. We're not in a hurry. Don't step on anything you can step over."

They headed into the woods north of the house slowly making their way toward the farmhouse and barns. The trees thinned out about one hundred meters from the house. Myra grabbed Joe's arm and got his attention. She gestured toward the nearest barn and nodded for him to leave. She moved away in the opposite direction to circle to the rear of the house.

Joe worked his way to the first barn. As he approached,

he could hear horses inside. The breathing and movement of the large animals was audible over the sounds of the night. Crickets and the occasional owl calling out to a mate provided a background for the staccato sounds from within the barn. Leaning against the wooden barn, Joe could hear the rhythmical breathing of the massive animals inside.

I wonder why they sleep standing up? thought Joe. *It must be a survival advantage.*

Joe decided nothing about this barn was unusual for a horse farm and moved toward the next outbuilding. He stopped and waited, looking both ways, before crossing the open ground between the structures. He slipped beneath the porch roof and knelt down watching for any movement. After a minute, he stood and cupped his hands on the glass windows. The interior was pitch dark. He found his flashlight in the pocket of his jogging suit and placed the lens against the glass. When he switched on the light, he could see equipment inside. His heart raced. There was a centrifuge in the corner. Binocular microscopes protected by plastic dust covers were on the tables. He could see a bank of modems blinking across the room. The equipment was first class. Polished chrome and stainless steel reflected back from his weak light.

This is definitely not what one would expect to find in a barn, thought Joe.

Joe felt the phone in his pocket vibrate. He instinctively reached for it and then thought better of it. It was a signal from Myra. He waited for a second ring. There was none.

I need to get the hell out of here.

Before he could finish the thought, a malevolent darkness settled over him as he crumpled onto the concrete porch.

Light was the first thing Joe sensed. The light hurt his eyes, so he closed them again. Then the pounding inside his head became the focus of his consciousness. He decided to move his legs, but couldn't. He painfully opened his eyes a slit and saw he was bound with duct tape. His left shoulder was numb from lying on it. Now it started to protest. He needed to move to allow circulation. Gradually, he began to hear voices penetrating the fog of hurt.

If I stay in this business, I need to get a helmet. This line of work is pretty demanding on your cranium.

Joe could hear the voices more clearly now. He continued to lie still and pretended to be unconscious.

"I got an email back from Oliver," said a voice Joe recognized. It was the man he talked with earlier that day.

"How do you like this, Paul? He said we should dispose of him," continued the man.

"That's what I think, too," said Paul. "He must have seen the equipment in the lab. We don't want him leaving here. If word gets out, the project is over. Our job is to protect the rear flank. It took a long time for someone to get this close, but we will make sure they don't get any closer."

"Do you think this guy was alone?" asked Carl.

"I don't know. If he knew anything, he would have brought help. I didn't see anyone, so maybe he is a lone wolf."

"He may just be a common thief, you know, looking for something to steal."

"I guess we'll find out soon enough. When he comes to, we can question him. You must have hit him pretty hard.

He's been out for almost six hours now. It's a wonder you didn't kill him."

"I might as well have killed him. He'll be dog food by tomorrow anyway. Paul, bring me another cup of coffee. I am responding to Oliver's email. I'm telling him to consider it done."

"We should load him in the trailer before the hired hands get to work. It's almost daylight and the boys will be comin' in soon. I'll bring the pickup around and we can carry him out while it's still dark."

"We've hauled a lot of Oliver's mistakes to the cannery, Paul, but this is the first time we've had to kill anybody. It didn't bother me much to do away with those poor animals that didn't turn out quite right, but killing a human being is another thing. I'm not too keen on this."

"I know what you're feeling, Carl. I don't like it either. Oliver has been right about everything so far," said Paul. "Maybe we just have to trust him. This thing is more important than us. What we're doing is going to change history. We can't stop now. We have waited centuries for this opportunity. We have to have courage. Remember our innocent brothers that were burned at the stake. We have to kill him before we throw him in the shredder. I can't bear to think about him being shredded alive."

"I agree. Wait 'till we get there. It's so noisy at the factory no one will hear anything. They are always shooting cows out back anyway."

"I'll go get the trailer. You start shutting the computer down and closing up the house. We need to get rid of his stuff. Someone will probably come out here looking for him. We will find a place to bury it tonight after everyone goes home. Maybe it would be easier to throw it in the river on the way back. No sense in keeping it on the farm for someone to find."

Paul opened the screen door and walked across the porch and into the semi-darkness. Carl sat down at the computer and logged out. He waited until the screen went dark to make sure it was completely off and then turned his attention to Joe lying on the rug in the corner of the room. Joe pretended to be asleep. Carl collected Joe's belongings and put them into the backpack. Joe heard the truck pull up next to the front porch.

"Pull 'er on by, Paul. Back the end of the trailer next to the steps. We won't have to carry him as far," Carl yelled out through the screen door.

He returned to Joe and began to try to roll him into a sitting position. Joe heard the screen door open.

"Com' on over here and help me get him up. He's heavier than he looks."

Suddenly Carl slumped on top of Joe and rolled off to one side. Joe opened his eyes and saw Myra standing over them holding the pellet gun by the barrel.

"I told you this would come in handy," she said cheerfully.

She pulled out the hunting knife and cut through the duct tape.

"Can you walk?"

"No, but I can run. Let's get the hell out of here before these guys wake up. Where's Paul?"

"I left him around back with a headache. He never saw me coming or he would have caught a BB in the eye. These guys are not that bright."

"I think you have been playing in the big leagues too long. They were plenty tough enough for me."

Myra pulled Joe to his feet and he put his arm around her shoulders as they walked out to the pickup. She opened the door on the passenger side and helped him in. She slammed the door, ran back into the house, grabbed his backpack, and flew out the screen door, across the porch, and into the truck. She jerked the shift lever into drive and the gravel flew as she accelerated down the long driveway. Turning left onto the hardtop, the four-horse trailer bounced across the cattle guard, swerving from side to side, and finally stabilized behind the pickup. Myra accelerated to sixty, hugging the centerline of the two-lane road as she negotiated the curves.

"You don't have any more of those little white pills, do you?" asked Joe hopefully.

"I have some in my pack. It is on the floor next to yours. Hand me my purse and I will get you one. How is your head?"

"It has a new lump. A phrenologist would have a field day with my skull."

"A what?"

"It's an inside joke. I'll tell you later. You drive. I'll find your pills."

"The sun is coming up, Joe. It's a beautiful day."

"You are definitely an optimist. I nearly get shredded and put into dog food cans, we are driving a stolen truck pulling a stolen horse trailer, and you wax philosophical about the glorious sunrise."

"I hate to tell you this, Joe, but I think we are being followed. There is a Jeep gaining on us and I think I recognize our friends."

"Drive faster."

I can't take the curves any faster with the trailer. The

thing weighs a ton and every time I swerve, it almost turns over. How do you feel, Joe?"

"Better. Why?"

"I need you to unhook the trailer. Can you get into the back of the pickup? Just open your door, swing around the cab, and climb into the bed. Can you do it?"

"Then what?" asked Joe suspiciously.

"Then you lean over the tailgate, unhook the safety chains, and loosen the trailer hitch knob. Can you do that?"

"A piece of cake," responded Joe sarcastically. "Is there anything else I need to do while I'm back there?"

"When you get the hitch loose, knock on the back window. I will slam on the brakes to take the tension off the ball and the hitch will probably separate."

"Probably?"

"Probably, Joe. There are no guarantees in my business."

"Do we have a Plan B?"

"No."

"Hold it straight down the road until I get out. I'll give it my best shot."

"Hurry, Joe. Our boys are gaining."

Joe opened the pickup door and held onto the safety belt as he swung around and put one leg into the bed. The door was banging against his right arm as he balanced with one foot in the cab and the other groping for the bed. He finally found a purchase with the fingers of his left hand on the back window rubber and pulled himself into the truck bed, falling clumsily. The door slammed against his right hand as he jumped, numbing his fingers. The cool air rushed by his face as he lay in the pickup and revived him. He rose and saw Myra's face in the rear view mirror. She was watching the road ahead and then looking at the side mirrors with concern. Joe looked over the side of the pickup bed and saw an open Jeep trying to overtake the trailer.

A shot of adrenalin hit him and he scrambled toward the tailgate. Leaning over the back, he saw the safety chains. He held onto a burlap bag of horse feed with his left hand for balance and unhooked both chains from the bumper. The safety chains bounced on the roadway, sparking, and leaping erratically. He grasped the feed sack firmly, leaned over the tailgate again, and began to unscrew the trailer hitch. His entire weight was supported by his chest against the top of the tailgate. Every bump in the road felt like it would break his sternum. He gripped the hitch and tried unscrewing it with his right hand. It was hard at first, and only moved a fraction of a turn. Gradually, it got easier and finally he unscrewed it completely. He rolled back into the bed, lying still until the pain in his chest subsided to a tolerable level, and then crawled on his hands and knees to the back window of the cab. He knocked. Myra motioned for him to get down. She slammed on the brakes and then accelerated. The trailer lurched and the hitch rose up off the ball and came free. The trailer started swerving from side to side, weaving down the road in ever-larger swings. Suddenly it turned sideways, flipped over, and started to roll.

The pickup started pulling away as the trailer slowed. Joe saw the Jeep swerve to the right to miss the rolling trailer and drive off the road. He could see Carl frantically trying to control the Jeep, but the ditch was too deep. The Jeep nosed into the steep embankment and rolled. Carl and Paul were thrown out of the rolling vehicle and lay motionless on the ground.

That will teach them to wear seat belts, thought Joe.

The trailer finally rolled to a stop in the ditch. Myra slowed the truck and stopped on the berm.

"Get in, Joe," shouted Myra.

Joe went over the side of the pickup and climbed into the cab.

"We have to go back to the farm, Joe. We need their computer. I should have brought it. I could kick myself."

Myra made a smoking u-turn and headed back to the farm. As they passed the Jeep, Myra saw Carl and Paul lying in the tall grass.

"I'll call the Highway Patrol as soon as we get some distance between us. Watch for the milepost signs. We need to give the police a location."

Myra pulled off the road when she got to her hidden car. She handed Joe the keys.

"Take my car and follow me to the farm," she said. "I'll grab the computer and anything else I think we can use and be waiting in the driveway. How are you feeling?"

"Those little white pills are good, boss. I will be right behind you."

Myra was waiting for Joe as he drove through the circular drive in front of the farmhouse. Joe left a cloud of dust as they turned onto the paved road and headed back toward the hotel.

"Where to from here, boss?"

"We need to find Oliver Henley. Carl was sending him emails, but that may not be enough for us to find him. We might find his address on the computer."

"I doubt it," replied Joe. "Henley is clever. I know someone who can find him, though."

"Who?"

"My good friend at the company, Ed Schultz. He does it for a living. He can find anything that has ever been on a computer. We have to get to D.C. I'll call him."

"Don't you dare, Joe. We are going to dump your phone. We use my phone from now on and my credit cards. Joe, someone is tracking your every move. We will grab our bags at the hotel and head for D.C. in my car."

Myra turned onto Loop 264 and pulled out her cell phone.

"I would like to report an accident on Farm-to-Market Road 22 West at mile post 34. There is an overturned Jeep and a horse trailer. It appears that two people are injured, maybe severely. You need to send an ambulance right away."

She hung up without giving her name.

CHAPTER 26

When they left the hotel, they took 64 east. Myra drove and Joe settled down in the front seat and began to relax.

"How is your head? You took a pretty good hit back there."

"I don't think I have a concussion. I'm feeling better. What are those little white pills you carry? That's good stuff."

"It's government issue. I don't know exactly what's in it, but it can definitely be habit forming. We can only get prescriptions for a limited amount. If you start taking it too frequently, you have to go to rehab. When you are in the field, you have to be able to function through a hell of a lot sometimes. We are supplied with a number of different drugs when we go out on an assignment. Sometimes it takes weeks to get back to normal."

"Myra, are you married?"

"No, and I never have been, if that's your next question. I do have a son, though. His name is Adam and he is just about the best son you could ever ask for. My mother takes care of him when I'm gone."

"And your father?"

"He died when I was twelve. He was my hero and still is. He was a great man, Joe. He was brave, smart, and loyal. I think of him every day."

"I guess you know about me, right?"

"I have to confess, Joe, I read your dossier. Your marriage didn't work out very well. Too bad."

"I wasn't ready for the big time, I guess. Kim was millennia ahead of me socially and I wasn't willing to try to change. I liked me as I was and she didn't. I know it's not any of my business, but there must be a story behind Adam. You don't seem to me to be a frivolous person. You wouldn't have had a child unless it was your decision."

"I wanted a child and I also wanted a career. More than a career, actually, I want to be the head of my organization. It was my father's dream, to be the head of the organization. He died a hero defending our country. I decided I would try to make his dream come true. I knew I couldn't have it all. No one can truly have it all. My mother was young enough to help me raise a child, so I decided to go to a clinic and get pregnant. I knew I wanted a son so I went to a fertility clinic. They can almost guarantee the gender of your child. Adam is the result. He's a fantastic son. He is kind, smart, and wise beyond his years. Pardon me, Joe. I'm going on like an idiot. I sound like every mother in the world."

"You are an amazing woman, Myra. I don't think I have ever met anyone that has your drive and ambition, and the ability to make it happen."

"Don't underestimate yourself, Joe. You came a long way from that farming town in the Midwest. You are an accomplished person. You had a good chance to win a Nobel. Very few people ever reach that level. Your social inexperience was you downfall, not your mind."

"I wasn't smart enough to avoid a disastrous marriage. Being married to a senator's daughter was just too tempting. I let Kim emasculate me."

"You aren't the first person to be corrupted by power. The moth being drawn to the flame is more than a figure of speech; there is a lot of truth to it."

"I see a truck stop up ahead. Let's get some coffee. We need gas anyway."

Myra pulled off onto the exit ramp and drove along the side road until she came to one of America's least elegant innovations, a combination gas station, convenience store, restaurant, gift shop, and cheap hotel. She pulled up to the pump and bounced out of the car.

"Whoa. I will pump gas," said Joe. "You find us some coffee and pay. You have the credit card, remember."

"Sounds like a deal to me," said Myra as she loped off to the store.

Joe filled the car with gas, checked the oil level, and cleaned the bugs off the windshield. Myra returned and handed Joe a Styrofoam cup.

"I think it is just the way you like it. Hand me your phone."

"OK, but why?"

"I overheard a trucker say he was on the way to California. I am going to give him a little something to take along."

Myra walked casually back across the parking lot until she came to a large Peterbuilt tractor belching black diesel smoke that was just starting to grind out of the lot toward the road. Staying out of the line of sight of the rear view mirrors, she jogged alongside and dropped the phone into the spare tire hanging beneath the trailer. She returned to the car with a grin.

"It will take them a while to figure that one out. I'll bet

your Cardinal O'Riley will be calling once he discovers the phone is heading west."

It was after dark as they approached Charleston, West Virginia. Joe had called Schultz on his Treō and set up a meeting for the next afternoon. Myra pulled off the highway and into a Holiday Inn.

"I'm beat, Joe," she said. "I didn't sleep last night. You still had your phone and I could follow what was happening in the farmhouse. Otherwise, I think I would have gone crazy. We need a good night's sleep if we are going to be sharp."

"I won't argue with that logic. Park this thing and we will hit the sack."

Myra rolled her suitcase up to the desk, pulled out her wallet, and put her credit card on the counter.

"I sure hope you have rooms left. We're beat."

"I think we can accommodate you tonight. Would you like one room or two?"

"One will be fine," answered Myra.

"King or two regulars?"

"A king would be nice," responded Myra, answering Joe's reflexive response with an almost imperceptible wink.

CHAPTER 27

"Wake up, sleepy head," were the first words Joe heard the following morning. He opened his eyes to find Myra standing beside the bed wrapped in a towel and fluffing her hair with another.

"I made coffee with the little pot in the bathroom. Get a shower. We have to hit the road. How is your head?"

"OK, OK. Good, I could use some coffee and my head is better," responded Joe sleepily.

He started to get out of bed and realized he was naked. Myra noticed his reticence.

"It's too late to be self-conscious," she said jokingly, as she dropped her towels and started pulling on her clothes.

"We have to get to D.C. by this afternoon. Your friend is expecting us, right?"

"Right," said Joe as he put a packet of sweetener into his coffee. "We have plenty of time to get there. What is the weather like?"

"Light rain and high in the low sixties. It's a great day for driving."

"Ever the optimist. What is good about light rain?"

"It's fun to watch the rain and listen to the sound of the windshield wipers as you drive. The rain cleans everything and the grass and trees look greener and happy. Rain is wonderful and renewing."

"My god, you sure make it hard to be grumpy. Try to restrain your enthusiasm and I will be ready to go in a jiff."

CHAPTER 28

It was almost midnight when the phone rang in the Intensive Care Unit of Saint Mary and Elizabeth Hospital in Louisville, Kentucky.

"Is this ICU?" intoned a very pleasant man's voice with a distinctive Irish accent. This is Father Hanratty. There are two members of my congregation on your ward and I would like to inquire about their condition. I believe you have a Carl Brundidge and Paul Warner. They were involved in a very severe automobile accident yesterday."

"We are not allowed to give out information regarding our patients except to family members. I am sorry, but it is hospital policy and I cannot make exceptions," was the crisp reply of the night nurse.

"I am in the lobby. I have been asked by the family to stop by. I am sorry to be so late, but I have had a long day. Many of my parishioners are experiencing problems and are in need of moral and spiritual support. I will be right up."

Before the nurse could respond, the phone went dead and she shrugged her shoulders.

What could it hurt? she thought. *Both of these guys were in pretty bad shape and, who knows, a little prayer might help.*

When the elevator on the ICU ward opened, Nurse Meg Jefferson was pleasantly surprised. The man that got off the elevator and walked up the long hallway was positively movie-star quality. He had an unruly shock of reddish blond hair and sparkling blue eyes. He was tall with broad shoulders and walked with a purpose. He was dressed in black and the white clerical collar and wooden cross were the only hints he was a man of the cloth.

Why are all the handsome ones either gay or priests, thought Meg Jefferson. *It's not fair.*

"Can you tell me where I can find Carl Brundidge and Paul Warner?" Hanratty asked setting his attaché case on the nurse station counter.

"As I told you, Father, we don't allow visitors except for immediate family and its well past our normal visiting hours."

"I have to tell you, Miss Jefferson," said Hanratty, glancing at her name tag, "God's work is not subject to a schedule. My poor souls in your unit do not have relatives that live in the area and I am the next of kin for all practical purposes."

He noticed the clipboard hanging on the chart rack. "I see Carl is in 343 and Paul is in 344. Which one is the most severely injured?"

"Mr. Warner has a broken arm, head injuries and possible internal. Mr. Brundidge has broken ribs, a broken leg, but he has an excellent prognosis. We will probably release him from the ICU when Doctor Krishnamurthy makes his rounds in the morning."

"I will visit with Carl first, then I can spend more time with Paul. He appears to be in greater need."

"Please don't awaken them, Father. They need rest."

"Thank you for your help, Miss. Jefferson. I think I can find my way."

Hanratty took his attaché case and disappeared into room 343.

Carl Brundidge was asleep or drugged when Hanratty pulled back the white curtains that separated patients on the ICU ward. His broken leg was hoisted on a trapeze and several electrical leads were attached to him that apparently provided information for the display monitors on the wall. A needle and interventions tube was connected to a liter bottle of fluid that dripped into his forearm. Hanratty knelt down by the bedside and stayed there until he heard the footsteps of Nurse Jefferson approach and then recede. He opened his attaché case and took out a syringe and small vial of medicine. He shook the medicine, removed the plastic sterilization cover, and inserted the needle through the rubber cap. He drew ten cubic centimeters of sodium pentothal from the vial and injected it into the intravenous tube. He watched the slightly different colored liquid as it crept slowly through the clear plastic tube and entered Carl's forearm. He checked his watch and waited. Presently, he shook Carl and began to awaken him.

"Carl, can you hear me?"

"I can just barely," Carl responded in a faint and slurred voice. "Who are you?"

"They sent me, Carl. You and Paul are hurt very badly. We have to take care of the farm, Carl. We need to have our people there in case someone comes poking around."

"I don't know you. Who are you?"

"Oliver sent me, Carl. He told me to come and help out. Carl, they took your computer. I can't contact Oliver. I need his number, Carl."

"They took the computer? How did they get it? I'm real

sorry. We tried to stop them. I think the girl hit me. I don't know where she came from."

"It doesn't matter now, Carl. You just need to get well. Tell me how to reach Oliver. I need to call him."

"You can't ever tell anyone his number. Promise me you won't ever tell anyone," said Carl though his drugged haze.

"You can trust me, Carl."

Hanratty held his small Sony digital tape recorder close to Carl's lips as he recited the numbers and addresses he had carefully memorized. Carl slowly faded into a deep sleep. Hanratty packed his briefcase and quietly left.

Sean Hanratty spent a short time with Paul Warner for the sake of appearance and then left the floor of the ICU. He thanked Nurse Jefferson profusely as he passed the nurse's station. She watched him with interest as he walked down the hallway and waited for the elevator.

Such a waste, she thought.

CHAPTER 29

The drive to D.C. was long, but the scenery was beautiful. They drove the interstates most of the day, crossing the Appalachian trial. Summer was almost most gone at the higher elevations and the leaves would be turning soon. Myra had been correct about the weather and the rain had been hard at times. The day passed too quickly. By the time they approached McLean, it was almost four o'clock. Joe called Ed and they agreed to meet at a Starbucks on Old Dominion Drive. Ed Schultz was sitting in his van when they pulled into the parking lot. He waived for them to join him. Joe and Myra dashed through the light rain, entered the van, and slid the side door shut.

"Ed, this is Myra. Myra, Ed. This is the computer genius I have been telling you about."

"Good to meet you, Myra. Joe didn't tell me you were beautiful as well as smart. Let's see this little puppy you are bringing me. Aha, a Sony Vaio. A little dated, but a good machine nonetheless. Did you try to log in?"

"It's password protected. I couldn't log in," replied Joe.

"The battery is low. I have a DC adapter. This should work," said Ed as he plugged a cord into the charging port.

"It's booting up. You're right. We need a password. It looks like there is some additional security software on this baby. First, I'll try this little cutie. It plugs into the USB port. I should be able to log in as administrator. It looks like it is going to work. Yep, we're in."

"Do you have it going already?" asked Myra. "Joe was right. You are a genius."

"Wrong. I just have the right tools. This is a piece of cake. Whoever set this up wasn't expecting a pro to try to break in. Most junior high students can get this far and just about as fast. What do you want to use for a password, Joe?"

"Let's make it 'JoeMyra'. I should be able to remember that."

"Now," asked Ed, "what do you want to know that's on the drive?"

"We are still looking for Dr. Oliver Henley," replied Joe. "You remember Henley? You were absolutely right. He's our man. We are pretty sure this computer contains information we need to find him."

"Let's do a search on Outlook," said Ed. "If there are any emails with Henley that should find them. Hmm, no Henley. They must be using a code name."

"I know this machine has emails from him," replied Joe. "I was present when one came into the mailbox. It should be one of the last ones that came in. The machine was shut down shortly after it arrived."

"There are several messages from a URL I don't recognize," said Ed as he scrolled through the Outlook folders. "I'll have to take this back to the office to track it down."

"You can't take the laptop into the office, Ed. We can't take any media into work, not even cell phones."

"Hide and watch, Joe. Just hide and watch. I do it all the time. I can't live at the office and I need to take things home to work on them. See this little memory card for a digital camera. If you fold it, it works in the USB port. Here, I'll show you. See?"

"OK. Now what, Ed?"

"First, I download the files from Outlook. O.K. Got them. Now we pull the card out and flatten it. Next, I slip it under the insole. I use these Comfort King insoles in all my shoes. I have narrow feet and these add a little more padding. I wear Rockports and they have rubber soles and a steel arch shank. The shank will shield the card in case they x-ray them. I carry it with me every day. The worst thing that happens is I get a slap on the wrist and a demerit if I get caught. We are not dealing with top-secret stuff here. If they fired everyone that took classified information out of the building, we would be out of business. Most of the files in the card are pictures of my family and MP3 files."

"How long will it take to find Henley's address?" asked Myra.

"I think I can break it down for you in an hour or less. I will leave the building before I call you. They monitor calls randomly and I don't want to take a chance on getting intercepted. I'll call Joe's Treō when I get something."

"Thanks, Ed. You can't imagine how much this means to us," said Joe.

"You have to promise to tell me what this is all about when and if you can. Myra, take good care of him. He looks better than I've seen him in years. You must be a good influence."

"I'm not sure I am a good influence, but I promise you I will try to take care of him."

Ed shook hands with Joe and patted him on the back as he left the van. Myra smiled.

Chapter 30

It was well before dawn in Rome when the phone rang in Cardinal O'Riley's bedroom. It took him several rings to realize the ringing was coming from the cell phone on the dresser and not the land line by his bed. O'Riley turned back the covers and groped for the dangling chain on his bedside lamp. The phone continued to ring persistently.

"Hello, Cardinal O'Riley here. Is this Sean?"

"Now, who did you think it would be, Cardinal, ringing you up on my own personal line?" came the irreverent response. "I have some interesting news for you about our man Henley."

"Great. I have some news for you, but I want to hear yours first."

"It seems your boy Joe has definitely located Henley. The farm has an entire research laboratory. The equipment looks expensive and there are several buildings that appear to be devoted to biological experiments. Lots of lab rats and horses. Apparently they were experimenting with horses. I'm pretty sure Joe was at the farm. I found some interesting things in the house like wrinkled duct tape with hair sticking to it and blood stains on the floor. Their computer is missing. There was a suspicious car accident about ten miles from the farm. Two men that work for Henley are in the hospital. One is in pretty bad shape and may not make it. You would be proud of me, Cardinal. I have been visiting the sick and offering a little spiritual support for our injured friends."

"Did you get a current address for Henley?"

"He's in Amsterdam. The company he works for is incorporated in the Netherlands. I am on my way to Cincinnati to catch a flight now. I think we can beat Joe to Henley if we hurry. Do you want to meet me there?"

"Definitely. I will get started as soon as I can get a plane. When do you arrive?"

"I can't get there until tomorrow morning. I pick up a KLM flight at Kennedy."

"I should be there by then. Meet me at the Grand Hotel Krasnapolsky. Do you know where it is?"

"Yea. I have been there before. Nice place. Just across from the old Royal Palace."

"That's it. I will reserve a room for you for early arrival tomorrow."

"What was your news, Cardinal?"

"It seems we have lost track of Joe. He hasn't called in two days and his phone signals are moving across the states, heading west. I think he planted the phone on someone to throw us off. His rental car turned up in the hotel parking lot in Louisville."

"Has he used his credit card lately?" asked Hanratty.

"No. He withdrew cash a couple of days ago, but not enough to pay for plane tickets or even hotels for very long. He seems to have dropped out of sight."

"Do you think he went home? Maybe he just decided to forget the whole thing. It's starting to get rough and Joe doesn't seem like much of a fighter."

"I don't know. It doesn't matter, Sean. He did his job.

We know about Henley and we know how to find him. We will finish this thing ourselves."

"I'll meet you at the hotel, Cardinal. I will call your room as soon as I arrive."

"Have a safe trip, Sean Hanratty. May God go with you."

CHAPTER 31

Joe and Myra were finishing a Big Mac and fries when the Treō rang. Joe swallowed the last bite and answered the call.

"Hi Ed. What did you find out? That's fantastic. I will call you later. Ed, you're the greatest."

"The server that Henley's emails are coming from is in Amsterdam," said Joe as he began to clean off the table. "They are located in a building owned by N.V.Trō Industries, incorporated in the Netherlands. They are the world's largest provider of in vitro fertilization services. The name is a play on words. The N.V. is the abbreviation for *Naamloze vennootschap* a legal term that literally means 'innominate partnership', the partners, that is, the shareholders, are not directly known. It makes sense these partners would prefer to not be known. Ed is texting me the address and phone number."

"I know that company, Joe. The clinic I used to have Adam is owned by N.V.Trō. They are supposed to be the best. I did a lot of research before I used them. We need to get to Amsterdam as soon as possible."

"You drive. I will call the airlines. Let's get started for Dulles. They have a ton of international flights. We should be able to find one tonight. Let's move it, girl. We are getting close."

The KLM flight to Amsterdam Schiphol took off on time at 10:30 p.m. The Airbus A340 rose quietly to cruising altitude and leveled off. Joe and Myra sat in Cabin Class in the center section of the wide body jet. They were squeezed into middle seats, bookended by exceptionally large companions.

"This must be a comedown from your last flight," Myra said into Joe's ear as she leaned against his shoulder. "I had to watch you from the back of the plane. You did quite a number on the vodka, as I remember."

"The vodka reciprocated," said Joe, grasping her hand. "I felt like hell the next day. Getting mugged in Louisville didn't help. I don't think I am cut out for this line of work. I have two lumps on my head the size of goose eggs and my hand is still sore from getting slammed in the door of the truck. My chest is black and blue from hanging over the tailgate and my joints are killing me from sleeping on the floor of the farmhouse wrapped up in duct tape, not to mention that I was almost dog food. You, on the other hand, are still in pristine condition."

"You should take better care of yourself, Joe. I wouldn't want anything to happen to you," said Myra with just a little sarcasm in her voice as she squeezed his hand.

"What are we going to do when we get to Amsterdam?" asked Joe. "Do we just go up to the receptionist and ask for Dr. Oliver Henley?"

"I've already checked the corporate web site. There is no Dr. Oliver Henley anywhere. My people at headquarters can't find him. We did a search for him as soon as you learned his name. Nothing after he finished graduate school. He just vanished. If he had been on the board of directors or an officer the company, he would have surfaced. We will have to think of something when we get there. I think he is the brains of this organization."

"Why?" asked Joe. "If he is such a big player, wouldn't he be an officer or on the board?"

"Not necessarily. He is too valuable to be a public figure. If he's driving the research, he would be too important to chance losing. Remember, the Knights Templar had a bad experience with the Catholic Church. Being burned at the stake for no particular reason would leave a lasting impression."

"It could leave a bad taste in your mouth," Joe agreed. "So how do we find the mysterious Dr. Henley?"

"We proceed carefully. I have to assume they know who you are. I don't think they know about me, yet."

"Why do you think they know me?" asked Joe in a surprised tone. "I haven't made contact with Henley."

"First, you have been asking questions about him for several weeks. You have found people that knew him. Buying information is a two way street. If someone can charge you for it, they could possibly charge the other party to tell them you are asking. We are not dealing with paragons of integrity here. Secondly, we have to assume Henley knew, or at least suspected, someone would find out about bribing Stancampiano and taking the relics. He paid big money for them. He wanted them very badly and would have tried to protect himself and the relics. He obviously had plans to do something with them. He sure didn't want anyone to stop him. Finally, we can't rule out the possibility someone in the Vatican is working for the Knights Templar. Someone must have gotten to Stancampiano in the first place, so we have to assume they still have someone inside."

"OK, now I feel stupid. What else can you tell me that I don't know?"

"When you have a man like Henley, you protect him. In the security business, we call it rings of security. Think of a big bull's eye, like a target. A head of state, for example, might have five or more rings. The target is the center and every ring gets harder to break through. The perimeter is the street cop. The last ring is the secret service agent who is willing to step in front of a bullet to protect the target. We are still on the periphery, not at the center."

"Considering how many injuries I have already suffered, I don't think I am going to last until we get to the bull's eye."

"Buck up, Joe. You are on the learning curve. You are a quick study and I am getting better at protecting you. Now, we need to get some sleep."

"Is your portable pharmacy open?" Joe asked hopefully. "I could use one of those little white pills."

CHAPTER 32

The phone rang in Cardinal O'Riley's room at the Hotel Krasnapolsky just as he was finishing unpacking his suitcase.

"You made it, Sean. Good. Take a few minutes to freshen up and I'll meet you in the Winter Garden downstairs. See you in ten minutes."

When Sean entered the *Wintertuin*, he scanned the room, but didn't see Cardinal O'Riley. As he was about to turn and head for the house phone, he saw a wave from across the room. He walked briskly toward the table and as he approached, he recognized the cardinal.

"I didn't expect to see you in a suit. You look more like an executive than a cardinal."

"I call my robes my traveling clothes. They always get me an upgrade to First Class. I change into a suit when I'm not going out to a public appearance. I am incognito. Without the robes, I am just another person and it's kind of nice occasionally. You would be amazed how much more you can learn about people if they don't know who you are. Did you get any rest on the trip over?"

"I slept most of the way. I needed it, too. I have been on the move since you called me last week. I'll have a stiff neck for a day or two from sleeping sitting up."

"I brought you a little present, Sean. It is in the briefcase by the table leg. Don't look down now. Just casually pick it up when we leave. No one will remember I carried it in."

"And I didn't bring you anything, Cardinal. I feel terrible," said Sean with a noticeable lack of sincerity. "What, may I ask, did you so generously decide to bring to this little gathering?"

"A Glock 9 mm automatic and two clips," said Cardinal O'Riley in a hushed tone. "Don't call me Cardinal. Call me Pat and keep your voice down."

"How in hell did you get through airport security with a pistol and ammo? It's almost impossible get a gun into Holland."

"It must be my traveling clothes," winked O'Riley. "When the alarm went off, I told security it was my gold crucifix. I told the young man the Holy Father had personally placed it over my head and I vowed not to take it off until I was called to my heavenly reward. He decided not to search me. I must have appeared to be trustworthy."

"Here is the plan, Pat. I'm going up to my room to shower and shave. We'll meet in the lobby about eleven. I want to walk by the N.V.Trō building a couple of times before lunch. Once we check it out, we will go to a café and talk. Don't walk too close to me and don't talk to me when we are scoping out the place. You don't know me, got it?"

"Then what, Sean? How do we find Henley?"

"I'm working on that. My plan now is for you go to reception and ask for a corporate brochure. Tell the receptionist you are on vacation from America and you represent a large organization. You saw their building and decided to come in and obtain some corporate information. Tell her your firm is always looking for progressive companies to invest in and you have heard good things about N.V.Trō."

"I can handle that. While I'm there I can look at the

building directory and see if his office is listed. If they ask for my card, I will tell them I am not authorized to reveal my company since I'm not on official business."

"I think you're getting the hang of this, Pat. I may be able to make you into a first class sleuth."

Sean picked up the briefcase and left the table. O'Riley signed the check and followed him to the elevators.

CHAPTER 33

The cab stopped in front of the Hotel Pulitzer in the heart of Amsterdam. The Pulitzer is comprised of about two dozen seventeenth century canal houses that line the Prinsengrach and Keizergrach canals. From the outside, it appears the houses are separate dwellings, but inside the architect has combined them into a modern five-star hotel.

"Very nice," said Joe as he pulled his carry-on up to reception. "Amsterdam was home to most of the sea captains during the Golden Age of Holland. Did you know the houses were taxed according to the distance they occupied along the canal? That is why they are so narrow and tall. The beam that juts out from the roof was used to support rigging, just like a ship, to hoist furniture to the upper floors. The stairs are too narrow."

"I didn't know I had my very own docent," replied Myra. "I can't wait for a tour of the red light district."

"Don't get your hopes up, little lady. My knowledge is gleaned strictly from reading and the books I grew up with were noticeably deficient in such matters."

Their top floor room had an excellent view of the heating system and air ventilators on the adjacent building. Wooden, hand-hewn beams formed the vaulted ceiling. Slate roofing tiles formed a ceiling mosaic. Wooden shutters swung from cast iron hinges were worn from centuries of use. The puddled glass in the windows was also original.

"I really love it, Joe. It's like going back in time. Do you think it is romantic?"

"I think it is romantic just being with you, Myra. In spite of my multiple injuries, I am having a wonderful time. I haven't been this alive in years. I just hope I stay that way."

Myra stood on her tiptoes and gave Joe a kiss on the cheek. Before he could respond, she darted away and began to explore the room.

"I get the first shower," she said as she began to shed her clothes. "You can unpack. I get the top dresser drawer and you can have the rest, OK?"

She didn't wait for an answer, as usual, and stepped into the shower humming a song Joe didn't recognize.

Joe yelled over the sound of the shower, "What do we do now? Do you have a plan yet?"

"First," Myra shouting over the thudding of the Water Pic, "we buy some different clothes. We will never blend in wearing the ones we have. There is a great flea market over on Waterlooplein. They sell everything there, especially used clothing. Nothing costs much more than a euro. It's about a ten minute walk from here."

When the water stopped, Myra stepped out of the shower and walked into the bedroom.

"Hurry it up, Don Quixote. It's time to go tilt at a windmill. We don't have all day. Amsterdam is an exciting place. We might as well enjoy being here. I'll be ready by the time you get out of the shower. Don't shave. Try to look disheveled."

"You should have seen me three weeks ago if you want disheveled. I'll be ready in no time."

The market on Waterlooplein stretched for several blocks. There must have been over a hundred stalls. The weather was good for Amsterdam, consisting of a slight drizzle and mostly cloudy skies. The stalls were covered with colorful tarps held down by bricks on ropes. A throng of customers, mostly tourists judging from their attire and polyglot conversations, shuffled up and down the street between rows of venders. The occasional outbreak of spirited haggling punctuated the murmur of the shoppers. The weather beaten faces of the vendors were tinged with an intriguing mixture of experience, guarded hope, resignation, and low expectations.

"What size do you wear, Joe? Here is a pair of jeans I like. They are just the right amount of 'worn out'."

"They look completely worn out to me, Myra. I threw away better jeans than that when I moved."

"I'll bet they didn't have the character these do. Hold them up. I think these will do perfectly. They need to have some pucker in the waistband. It will appear you have lost weight. Try on this belt. I can put another hole in it if it's too big. Now, you need a sweatshirt, preferably with something written on it in Cyrillic letters. Here's one."

"What does it say? Can you read it?"

"It's a beer advertisement. Don't worry, it doesn't say anything bad."

"Why don't I trust you?" said Joe smiling.

"These shoes are right. Try them on."

"I think I will keep my shoes, if you don't mind."

"Wrong, Joe. Shoes are the most important piece of any disguise. Eastern European shoes are made of cheap leather and they have this really gross stitching. You can spot a shoe made in Bulgaria or Russia a mile away. They are a must for this look. Now, all we need are white work socks."

Myra found Joe a warn leather jacket and then started shopping for herself. Joe watched as she stopped at several stalls, carefully examining the clothing. She finally decided on a pair of tight jeans, a wide belt, a shirt that buttoned down the front, a fitted leather jacket, and a pair of black boots with three-inch heels. She also purchased several pieces of cheap looking jewelry to compete her ensemble.

"I think you got the best of this shopping spree, Miss Myra. You are going to look quite smashing in those garments and I am going to look more like a street bum."

"It will work out, Joey. Just trust me."

"You keep saying that, but I'm not getting any more confident."

"Let's go back to the hotel and change," said Myra. "We have things to do. Our first order of business is to get you a working cell phone."

CHAPTER 34

Cardinal O'Riley walked down Spuistraat until he arrived at number 1307. The building holding forth at that location was distinguished only by the incredible sameness of its features. Scores of small, identical windows were arranged in a rectangular pattern in a wall of small, dingy red bricks. The building was over ten stories in height and was shaped like a giant shoebox. On the northwest end was a small portico with a sign that subtly advertised a Reijksbank was concealed inside. He walked by the entrance and peered intently inside as he came even with the glass doors. He saw only his own reflection in the doors. They were covered with reflective Mylar.

On the return pass, he stopped, pretended to scrutinize the sign above the portico, climbed the steps, and entered. He approached the well-groomed young lady behind the mahogany reception desk and spoke in his most resonant and authoritative voice, "I am told there is a company by the name of N.V.Trō at this location. I do not seem to find the name on your directory. Can you tell me the floor on which they are located?"

"I am not familiar with that firm, sir. Perhaps you have an incorrect address."

"Are you certain? I am sure this is the address. I am from America and I represent a large firm that does business worldwide. We are always looking for investment opportunities in leading technology firms. It is my understanding N.V.Trō is a leader in its field."

"I wish I could help you, sir, but I can assure you there is no such company at this address."

"Thank you very much, anyway. I am very sorry to have bothered you, miss. Now I shall get back to my holiday. 'Nothing ventured, nothing gained' is my motto. Good day."

As the door closed behind O'Riley, the receptionist picked up her phone and began keying in a number.

O'Riley left the building and continued down Spuistraat until he reached Paleisstraat. Turning right, he headed across Dam Square. He could see the Hotel Krasnapolsky ahead when Sean overtook him.

"Let's have a glass of wine, Pat. Shall we?" suggested Sean coming up alongside. "How did it go back there?"

"There is no such company at that location, Sean. Your information is bad. We are on a wild goose chase."

"I don't think so, Pat ol' boy. I was there when Carl was giving me the address and, unless he is up for an Academy Award this year, he was telling the truth. These Knights Templar are no fools. 'Burn me once, shame on you. Burn me twice, shame on me'."

O'Riley opened his mouth as if to defend the Church, but could think of nothing to say. He motioned for Sean to enter the Winter Garden bar at the Hotel Krasnapolsky. They sat at a table by the window.

Cardinal O'Riley leaned across the table and asked, "What now, Sean? How do we find this Henley?"

"A good question, your Eminence. I think we watch the building for a while. You are known, now. I'm sure they have your picture on the security cameras. I am still anonymous. We have to keep it that way. We can't be seen together in public. We will meet in the hotel only. Call my cell if you need to talk. I am going to do a little reconnoitering. I'll call you when I return to the hotel. You go do a little sightseeing. That will at least lend some credibility to your cover story."

CHAPTER 35

Joe and Myra raised a number of eyebrows as they exited through the lobby of the Hotel Pulitzer dressed in their new attire. Hotel guests, assuming they were probably employees leaving for the day, wondered why they didn't' use the employee entrance. Employees assumed they were from one of the former soviet countries and had not yet grasped the subtleties that accompanied wealth. Amsterdam is, without doubt, the most tolerant city in the world. Individual freedoms and eccentricities are seemingly embraced more than tolerated. Whenever interest is aroused, which is not often, it is typically curiosity tinged with a degree of covet for not having thought of it first.

Once on the streets, Myra and Joe did not elicit a second glance. They talked incessantly, walking through the crowded streets and interconnecting pedestrian passageways. They window shopped at upscale department stores and noted the sex shops, peep shows, and sidewalk cafes in the tourist district. The aroma wafting from cafes was definitely not from plants discovered by Sir Walter Raleigh in the New World. Their origin was definitely Old World.

"Let's get a cup of coffee," said Myra stopping outside a busy cafe. Myra pointed out the various herbs one could order from the menu.

"I've read about this," said Joe, "but I never really thought it would be this blatant. The patrons of this cafe are very well behaved and not disruptive at all. In fact, they seem downright placid. Getting high is much cheaper here than in America."

"Once you legalize something," added Myra, "the price comes down because you reduce or eliminate the risk to the supplier. Supply and demand are the keys to cost. The price of drugs settles down to the cost of production and distribution and the demand regulates supply. The taxman gets his share which more than pays for enforcement of the rules. Capitalism is a very interesting concept when allowed to operate freely. It's when people try to introduce religion, societal mores, and hypocrisy into the mix that it seems to get complicated."

"I think I like Amsterdam," declared Joe. "Holland has always been a safe haven for radical thinkers. Spinoza lived here and so did René Descartes, Pierre Boyle, and John Lock. The all came here to exchange ideas. The Vietnam War had a similar effect. It is no wonder the Knights Templar chose Amsterdam as home base."

"I remember Descartes from philosophy class. 'I think, therefore I am' if I remember correctly. Is that right?"

"Right you are, Myra."

"We can't forget Dylan, Joey," said Myra grinning mischievously. "'Don't think twice, it's all right'."

"Myra, you're hopeless."

"Speaking of the Knights, Joey, shall we take a look at the building? It's just down the street from here."

"I have nothing better to do, unless, of course, you would like to return to the Pulitzer for a brief interlude. I must say you look very comely in your new used clothes."

"Hold that thought, Joey. Let's take a look at the

building first. We can discuss our plan of attack at a later time in more comfortable attire and surroundings."

As they approached the building, Myra leaned over to whisper into Joe's ear, "Walk on ahead. I don't want to advertise the fact we are together. I will wait until you get to the next block before I follow. Continue two more blocks then wait for me to catch up."

"Got it, boss."

Joe strolled casually past the Reijkstad Bank building and noticed the doors were opaque. He found nothing of note to remember to tell Myra. Stopping at a self-serve newspaper rack, he pretended to read the headlines through the scuffed plastic window. He saw Myra had crossed the street and was standing in the Plexiglas tram shelter as if waiting.

Good thinking. She has located a vantage point for us. Why didn't I think of that?

Myra watched the entrance to the brick building for a short time, then walked briskly on down the street, soon overtaking Joe's ambling stroll.

"Are you sure about the location, Joe? This building looks pretty damn sterile to me."

"I'm sure. First, Ed doesn't make mistakes like that. If he says this is the location of the email servers, then I would bet my life on it. Secondly, did you notice the address?

"Of course. It's 1307 Spuistraat. Why?"

"The Knights Templar were burned at the stake in 1307. Now, let's go back to the Pulitzer and figure out what we do next."

"I think I know exactly what you have in mind, Joey. Then we can get down to business."

Joe pulled Myra a little closer and she laid her head on his shoulder. They stared up at the beams in the ceiling of the Pulitzer sharing their warmth.

"Do you ever wish you smoked?" asked Joe patting her shoulder. "In movies they always light up about this time."

"Maybe we can just pretend to smoke," giggled Myra. "It's better for your health and you don't burn holes in the sheets."

"It's cheaper, too. Would you hand me my sterling silver Tiffany cigarette case and that Cartier table lighter on the bedside stand? I shall, of course, offer you one first."

"I believe you are a true gentleman, sir. I am pleased to make your acquaintance."

"Kidding aside, Sherlock Jr., what do we do next? You are the brains of this outfit. Do you have a plan?"

"Well, Dr. Watson, we are back to watching and hoping for a break. We could take the frontal approach and go into the offices with some hokey story that might get one of us a meeting with Henley. Another plan would be to break in at night and look for evidence, but that building is huge. We don't have a clue as to where to start looking. I'm sure they have excellent building security and since we put their farm team in the hospital, they will be expecting someone. Could you recognize Henley from the description you have?"

"I don't know, truthfully. The only people I talked to haven't seen him for twenty years. He's aged and he may have changed his appearance. Who knows what he looks like now?"

"Here is the plan. It's weak, but it leaves us options for

later. We are going to watch the entrance for the next few days. You will stay in the tram stop. I will hover around the area watching for any signal from you. We can think of something with a newspaper or some object I can spot from a block away."

"What am I looking for?" inquired Joe.

"As I have told you before and I'll tell you again, you are looking for something unusual, suspicious, extraordinary, or just plain strange. If we don't get any results, we will try Plan B."

"But, right now we don't have a Plan B, correct?"

"Correct. So let's make Plan A work, shall we?"

Chapter 36

The typically Amsterdam cloudy and drizzly weather held. Joe spent the next day in the tram stop pretending to wait for a ride. He arrived just after dawn and stayed until nearly dark. The entrance to the Reijksbank was busy in the morning and evening, but slowed to a trickle during business hours. The pattern suggested daytime employees coming and leaving their workplace. There was little traffic during banking hours, indicating the bank was not serving traditional customers.

It was almost seven o'clock when a black Mercedes pulled up in front of the bank and parked. The water vapor from the exhaust indicated the car was idling. Suddenly, the front door of the bank opened and a tall man, ramrod-straight and impeccably dressed, gracefully descended the steps, opened the rear passenger door, and got in. The car sped off.

Joe was almost too mesmerized to react. Picking up his folded newspaper, he began slapping it against his leg, the signal for Myra to approach. She came into the enclosure and stood next to Joe facing the opposite direction.

"I saw him, too. He could just be our man."

Before Joe could respond, he was thrust against the Plexiglas wall and pinned. Joe looked up into the face of his attacker. He was in his late twenties and had greasy, dirty blond hair. His teeth were yellowed and his beard was sparse and too light to make much of a statement. He leaned against Joe, using his weight and height advantage, and began speaking in a harsh language Joe did not comprehend.

"Hold on, guy. I am just waiting on the next car. Back off," Joe sputtered.

Switching to Pidgin English, the attacker shouted, as if to make himself understood, "This my territory. You get out. Take your whore and leave."

Myra tapped the thug on the shoulder and said something in what could have been the same guttural language. The attacker turned to face Myra. Joe could see she had unzipped her coat and her shirt was open down to where it was tied around her waist. The big man smiled and reached out with his right hand.

Before his hand touched Myra's chest, she grabbed his index and middle fingers with her right hand and cupped his elbow with her left hand. He could not jerk out of her grasp. The attacker stood on his toes grimacing, trying to relieve the pressure from his fingers. He towered above Myra, but was no longer a threat. A sickening crack ensued. The fight was clearly gone from him and his eyes darted around for an escape that didn't exist. Myra leaned toward his face and spoke to him quietly in his language. He nodded affirmatively and she slowly released his fingers. He was gone as quickly as he appeared.

"What the hell was that all about?" said Joe as they walked back to the hotel.

"He thought I was your whore and you were cutting into his territory. Apparently he is the local pimp for this area."

"What did you say to him? I think you broke his fingers."

"I believe they are just badly sprained. Sometimes it's difficult to get it just right. I told him you were Special Forces and just out on a psycho discharge. I told him you were the first Afghanistan Rambo."

"Do you think he'll come back tomorrow?" asked Joe.

"No. Bullies are typically cowards. He will wait until we leave and then reclaim his territory. What did you think about the man who left in the limo?"

"I think that was Dr. Henley, Myra. He fits the description. He has a military bearing. What do we do now?"

"Let's go back to the hotel and think about it, Joey. I believe you are right. That was probably our man. We need to figure out what we do next, now that we may have found him."

CHAPTER 37

The phone in Cardinal O'Riley's room rang just as he was about to call Sean.

"How did it go today, Sean? Yes, I can come to your room immediately. I'll be right there. Goodbye."

"Good evening, Pat," said Sean as Cardinal O'Riley allowed the door to the room to close behind him. Would you care for a little good Irish whiskey? Come over to the desk and look at my pictures. I used your American Express card to buy myself a nice camera today. It has a very good telephoto lens."

"You are only authorized to spend money on the case, Sean. Those are the rules. This is the Church's money, not ours to spend on frivolous toys."

"This is for the cause, Pat. I downloaded the photos to my laptop. See this guy waiting to catch the tram? Do you know him?"

"I never saw him before in my life, as far as I know. Am I supposed to know him?"

"Let me enlarge it for you. Now do you recognize him?"

"Well, I'll be. It's Joe McPherson. I would never have recognized him in those clothes. How did you spot him?"

"He's been watching the bank for the last couple of days. I think he is with a girl. I can't be sure, but she hangs out in the general area. I saw him talking to her several times.

When I questioned Carl back in Louisville, he mentioned something about a girl being with Joe. She could just be a whore, but I think they know each other."

"What do you think we should do, Sean? Do we confront him?"

"No, not now. We watch him. If he finds Henley, we find Henley. He probably knows more than we do. He has the building staked out. I will watch him and the girl. You stay out of sight. He might recognize you and then we lose our edge. You better rent a car. Better still, get a van. We might need room to carry a body or two. Vans are less conspicuous anyway. Try to get one that doesn't look like a rental. Try to find one of those Rent-A-Wreck places. There must be some cheap rentals here in Amsterdam with all the dope heads running around."

"Sean, we have to find Henley and stop him immediately. The future of the Church depends upon it. God has called me to lead at this most critical time in history. The Lord has chosen me to save our sacred Church. I will be revered throughout history as a Defender of the Faith."

CHAPTER 38

Joe was in the tram stop at dawn the next morning. At seven sharp, the same black Mercedes pulled up in front of the building and the rear passenger door opened. The tall man got out, leaned inside the car, and said something to the driver. The man was carrying a brown leather briefcase. He strode confidently up the steps, taking them two at a time, and entered. While Joe was watching him enter the building, the car sped off. By the time Joe remembered to watch where the car went, it was out of sight.

Boy, I'm a lousy spy, Joe thought as he cringed inside. *I didn't see the man's face, the license number, and I don't even know which way the car turned when it left. It's a good thing I was a decent biologist.*

Joe looked around for Myra. Not seeing her anywhere, he sat down on the bench pretending to read his newspaper.

I better make sure I hold it right side up, he chided himself. *This would make a good Pink Panther movie with me playing Inspector Clouseau!*

"Don't turn this way," came a familiar voice from behind. "Just stare straight ahead. Did you get a good look at his face?"

"No. He was turned the other way. I don't have twenty-ten vision either. Did you get the license plate number?"

"Yes. I have it memorized. I will call headquarters later and check it out. I doubt it will lead anywhere. The car will be back to pick him up. We have to be ready to follow him. I would be surprised if Henley left before five or six this afternoon. He seems to be a workaholic. However, we can't assume he will stay here all day. I will go get transportation so we can follow him when he leaves. You keep watching. I'll bring you coffee and a sandwich later."

The steel gray skies were beginning to darken and the wind off the Zuiderzee blew cold and damp. Joe watched the building intently, knowing it was nearing the time when the black Mercedes should be arriving. Joe looked up and down the street, hoping to catch glimpse of Myra. He felt vulnerable when she was not there. He looked back at the building just as the Mercedes limousine rolled to a stop. Joe pushed the speed dial on his phone. It seemed like eons until the phone rang.

"He's here. Hurry. They're just pulling away."

Joe watched the Mercedes accelerate into traffic and then turn right at the next corner. A black Ducati Streetfighter roared up to the tram shelter and screeched to a stop.

"Jump on, Joey. It's show time," yelled Myra as she flipped down her helmet visor.

Joe threw his leg over the back of the motorcycle and grabbed the helmet hanging on the seat clip. He almost slid off the jump seat as the motorcycle accelerated and bounced across the tram tracks in pursuit of the Mercedes. Joe pulled on the helmet with one hand and held onto Myra with the other.

"Hold on with both hands and lean when I do. Lean into the turns and hang on tight. We can't afford to lose them now."

Driving between the lanes of traffic, Myra quickly made up the distance. The Mercedes headed out of Amsterdam toward Aalsmeer. Myra maintained almost a kilometer separation behind the Mercedes as they sped by green fields. They passed the exit to Aalsmeer. Overhead signs indicated that Leiden was the next town of any size. Joe zipped up his jacket and tucked in behind Myra. He could feel her body tense with excitement as she guided the motorcycle along the smooth highway. She tailgated the car in front of them, to stay out of sight of the Mercedes.

Joe saw the Mercedes signal to turn off the divided highway and immediately Myra downshifted to slow the Ducati. By the time they arrived at the exit, only the taillights of the Mercedes could be seen. Myra cut the headlight and they tailed the Mercedes for another ten minutes. The flicker of the brake lights indicated the Mercedes was slowing or turning. Myra pulled off the road onto the soggy ditch and waited. When she had allowed enough time, she accelerated toward a junction in the road ahead. As they topped the knoll, they saw a gravel driveway that branched off the hard surface road. When they came abreast of the driveway, the interior lights lit as the doors opened. The Mercedes sat in the driveway of a large, stone farmhouse. Myra upshifted into second, keeping the engine of the motorcycle to an idle, and continued past the driveway.

"What is that awful smell?" asked Myra.

"This is a dairy farm, my little city girl. A cow is an animal that turns grass into manure. Milk is a by-product of the process. The smell comes along for free."

Myra gently accelerated the Ducati and continued down the road. Large rolls of newly bailed hay sat in the fields by the roadside. Myra pulled onto the grass and Joe cheerfully jumped off the back. She guided the Streetfighter behind one of the large bales and propped it against the hay.

"We go on foot from here," she said taking off her helmet and hanging it on the handlebar. "We will work our way along the fence and then cut over to the house. Stay low. Try not to provide a profile. It will be pitch dark soon. The clouds are thick and the moon won't be a factor tonight."

Myra took one last look up and down the highway and then ran in a crouch toward the white fence on the other side. Joe dutifully followed. They worked their way along the fence line until they were approximately one hundred meters from the house. Myra kneeled by a fence post and motioned for Joe.

"There is a light in the downstairs window and the front porch light is on. We will approach from the back of the house and try to get a look inside. Wait until I get across the yard and into the bushes by the window. Then follow my path. Don't make a sound. Is your phone off?"

"It's on vibrate."

"Turn it completely off. You can hear those things vibrate for fifty feet."

"Maybe you can," replied Joe.

Myra giving him a disapproving look, vaulted nimbly over the fence, and ran to the rear of the house. Joe lost her in the darkness as she melted into the bushes. Joe climbed over the fence heading for the bushes where Myra had disappeared. As he reached them, a hand grabbed him by the collar and pulled him into the shrubs.

"I told you to be quiet," whispered Myra. "You sounded

like a Clydesdale coming across the yard. Move over to that window. There is light inside the room."

They crept through the bushes until they were beneath the large window. The scale of the house was not evident until they were standing beside it. The stone walls were almost a meter thick and the window sill jutted out from the wall. Joe was a foot shorter than the glass at its lowest point. Myra looked up in frustration.

"Bend over. I'm going to get on your shoulders. That is the only way I can see inside."

Joe squatted and Myra leapfrogged onto his shoulders. He used his hands against the stone wall for balance as he stood erect. Myra was just able to peer into the lower panes.

"Can you see anything?" whispered Joe.

"Why don't you come inside and join us?" boomed a voice from behind them. "You will be able to see much better. We don't get much company out here, you know."

CHAPTER 39

Joe turned around slowly with Myra still perched on his shoulders. In the dim light from the window, they saw a well-dressed man they recognized as the driver of the Mercedes. He was holding a gun with a satisfied smile on his face. Joe started to lower Myra.

"Just stay the way you are," their protagonist intoned. "I want Dr. Henley to see this. Besides, you won't get far if you decide to run with her on your back," he laughed.

Myra ducked as they entered the front doorway, but the high ceilings inside the house provided ample space for them as they walked down the entry hall and entered the living room. A fire was burning in the carved stone fireplace. Over the mantle was the unmistakable coat of arms of the Knights Templar.

As Joe's eyes slowly became accustomed to the light level, he saw bookcase lined walls filled with an eclectic collection of books and art. Comfortable leather chairs were arranged in a wide circle around the fireplace. A huge Persian rug completed the decidedly masculine décor.

"You may put her down, Dr. McPherson," said the tall, distinguished man standing by the fireplace. "Thank you, Jurgen, for giving me the opportunity to observe our visitors in stalking mode."

Jurgen expertly frisked both Joe and Myra and nodded to Oliver Henley they were unarmed. Jurgen stood by the entrance holding his gun by his side. Henley motioned for

Joe and Myra to come forward. A third man, who Joe did not recognize, sat in a chair near the fire.

"I am Oliver Henley, Dr. McPherson," said the tall man. These are my associates, Jurgen and Claus. If you don't mind, please introduce your lovely companion.

"This is Myra Cohen. She is a friend and has no involvement in this. I met her in Amsterdam."

"Very chivalrous of you, Dr. McPherson, but from my information she is very much involved in your schemes to locate me. I must congratulate you on your resourcefulness. I truly did not think it was possible to track me down after all these years. You are obviously very intelligent not to mention persistent. I have read your published papers. Even though the work was done before you joined the CIA, they are brilliant. I cannot imagine why you abandoned such a promising career to work for the American intelligence agency. You were essentially buried alive intellectually."

"It's a long story, Dr. Henley."

"May I offer you a glass of wine, brandy, or perhaps something stronger?"

"It's very tempting," replied Joe, "but I'll pass. You wouldn't have any strong coffee, would you?"

"Unfortunately, no," replied Oliver Henley. " We drink tea. Sorry. You are probably wondering why I allowed you to come here. The reason is simple. Ego. I have succeeded in performing a scientific miracle of sorts and I don't have anyone who can truly appreciate it to share it with. Do you realize how frustrating that can be? I cannot publish my work and I will never be recognized for my achievement. It's like getting a hole in one when you are playing alone or running the billiards table and no one is watching, only much more important. It is my life's work and there is no one to appreciate it."

"Is your offer of a drink still open?" asked Myra. "I could use a brandy."

"Of course. Please excuse my manners. As I said, we don't get many visitors. Claus, will you pour Miss. Cohen a drink? Sit down and enjoy the fire. I am an ungracious host."

"If I may ask, how are your men in Louisville?" inquired Myra.

"Very kind of you to ask, Miss Cohen. They are both on the mend. I apologize for their heavy-handed treatment, but we weren't sure how many people were involved in this or who they were."

"I would like very much to hear about your research, Dr. Henley," entreated Joe. "I assume you have succeeded in creating a clone from the relics you obtained from Cardinal Stancampiano."

"Actually, Dr. McPherson, that is incorrect. I never had any intention of creating a clone of Jesus Christ."

"Then, why did you go to all the trouble to obtain the relics from the Vatican, the hair and blood samples?"

"My research concentrates on another aspect of genetic engineering," continued Dr. Henley. "I have always been more interested in gene splicing. When I was an undergraduate student, I developed a keen interest in horses. Even then, we recognized it might be possible to clone an animal or human being, for that matter. The problem with cloning, especially if you are a horse breeder, is you produce an animal that is an exact replica of its progenitor. If I clone Secretariat, for example, I get a young Secretariat or maybe a dozen Secretariats. If I create an identical horse, I haven't improved the bloodline. Besides, who wants to watch a field of identical horses run for the Kentucky Derby?

"I see your point, Doctor," responded Joe. "The interesting thing about a horse race is the unknown factor. The diversity of the field drives the betting and the interest. A very good point."

"Further," continued Dr. Henley, "there has never been the perfect horse. Every animal has flaws. If you compare all the Triple Crown winners, you will find advocates for every one of them as well as their detractors. That, as they say, is what makes it a horse race."

"So what is your solution, Dr. Henley?" said Joe. "How do you solve this conundrum?"

"Please call me Oliver, Joe. My solution is quite simple in theory, yet extremely complex in practice. I decided to attempt to identify the genes that made a great horse great. If I could do that and combine them into a single animal, I could develop a superior species. This is exactly what breeders do, as you know. They cross-breed animals that have complementary characteristics, a great mare bred to a champion stud. However, the breeding process is like rolling the dice with the gene pool. You will get some combination of genes, but probably not the most desirable one. Further, you only have two sets of genes with which to work."

"And how do you solve this most ancient of problems?" asked Joe.

"As I said, my solution was simple. I had to identify genes that produce the desirable traits and splice them into another, near perfect animal. Further, it is possible to combine the superior characteristics of several animals; for now the mare, the stud, and the spliced genes. I refer to it as the triple cross. When the added traits are dominate, the result is a super species. Further, as you continue to develop the bloodline, you can add more desirable characteristics. I became proficient enough to make a very good living. I cannot create a perfect animal yet, but I am light years ahead of random breeding."

Joe leaned forward, his elbows on his knees, now totally engaged.

"How do you identify the specific genes that develop into the desired traits?"

"That, Joe, is the crux of the matter, isn't it? I hope you don't mind if I call you Joe. I tried for years to find a way to locate the exact segment I wanted. I had to find the entire sequence, not too much, not too little. That is where the one percent inspiration comes in. Ninety-nine percent of research is just hard work, perspiration. We need that one percent of inspiration to get past the seemingly impossible hurdle. My solution was to develop a gene marking technique that did not cause mutation, but would survive as the embryo developed. I had already developed methods of approximately locating the sequence in the genome. My gene marking technique allowed me to mark the sequences, grow the embryo, and then verify experimentally I had selected the correct sequence. The procedure was rather crude at first, but with enough trials, I was able to perfect it. I started with rats, of course. The gestation period is so short I could turn experiments around in days. As I became more successful, I used other small animals and then horses."

"Don't you think it is unethical to create such test tube animals?" asked Myra. "This process of yours gives you an unfair advantage over the other breeders. It's like an athlete taking steroids."

"First, I am not concerned with the ethics of biology. That is for others to argue. I am a scientist and I want to push the limits of science. Secondly, I am only hastening what hundreds of years of selective breeding could accomplish. Finally, you can appreciate the fact that this process can help eradicate diseases that have plagued humankind forever. Virtually every major scientific innovation is greeted with skepticism. Why wouldn't we want our children to have a better life than we have?"

"This brings me back to my earlier question, Oliver. Why did you go to the trouble of obtaining the relics of Jesus Christ?" asked Joe earnestly.

"When you are invited to join the Brotherhood of the Knights Templar, you must take a vow that has been passed down for hundreds of years to avenge those who were sacrificed by the Church. We believe the Church became corrupted by power and lost sight of the mission God intended. Our crusade is to restore the true meaning of Christianity, which is to make the world more Christ like."

"When I realized it might be possible to recreate the essence of Jesus Christ, I went before the Ruling Elders of the Knighthood and proposed we obtain enough of the relics of Jesus to at least attempt to discover if there was a perceptible genetic different. When we take the Oath of Knighthood, we are told about the existence of the relics, the sacred relics that we, the Knights Templar, discovered in Solomon's Temple and gave to the Church as a symbol of our loyalty."

"And so you were given the mission to obtain the relics

and try to unravel the mysteries of Jesus' power?" added Joe.

"That is correct. I had already begun my experiments with horses and it appeared to be a funding source. The Ruling Elders like to make a profit, just as any board of directors. That is how we maintain our power. I was allowed, even encouraged, to use profits from my genetic breeding projects to finance the Jesus Christ experiment. The techniques I developed for genetic breeding became so successful I was directed by the board to commercialize them. We spun off N.V.Trō soon afterward which quickly grew into a very successful and profitable venture."

"Surely you didn't experiment with the relics by trial and error. I can't imagine creating embryos and then destroying them," injected Joe.

"I would never think of doing such a sacrilegious thing," responded Oliver. "I had acquired very powerful computers by that time. They were capable of sequencing the genome of the relic samples and comparing the results to the human genome. The outcome was astounding."

"How so?" asked Joe, now completely engrossed.

Henley drew closer to Joe and in almost breathless tones, he continued, "I found a new sequence that did not exist in the human genome. It is different from anything I have ever seen before. I couldn't find anything even similar to compare it against. I decided to call it the JC sequence. I believe it is what differentiates God from men."

Joe sat back in his chair and stared into space, contemplating the enormity of what he had just heard then asked, "Are you completely sure?"

"As you know, a scientist is trained to be a skeptic. I tried every other possible explanation and checked my work time and again. I reproduced the result many times and there was no difference. The only thing I do not have is an independent researcher to verify my work. I will not be completely satisfied until someone else can duplicate my experiment."

"What, may I ask," said Myra, "did you do with this incredible discovery?"

"I did something very bold, Myra," replied Oliver. "I decided to propagate the gene sequence in others to determine what effects it has on a human being."

"Without their knowledge!" responded Myra emphatically. "That is definitely unethical and probably illegal. You can't dabble in other people's lives without their consent. How did you get your subjects?"

"They were our customers in N.V.Trō. We have clinics all over the world. Every time we implanted the eggs we had fertilized from a donor, they contained the JC gene splice. It was built into the process."

"Dr. Henley," said Myra, her voice betraying her outward calm, "my son was conceived at your clinic in Tel Aviv. Does he have the gene splice?"

"How old is he now?" responded Oliver.

"He is almost twelve. He will be twelve in three months."

"It is very possible he does," said Oliver in an almost clinical tone. "Tel Aviv was one of the first locations to get the process. I thought it would be ironic to introduce the gene in Israel first. Also, the patients are almost entirely Jewish and it is only fitting the Jews have the opportunity to produce another Jesus Christ."

"How can I find out!" demanded Myra. "I am entitled to know if you have changed my son in a way that could be harmful to him. What if this gene splice you have added turns out to cause serious problems as he gets older? You had no right to interfere in something as sacred as creating a human life!"

"First," replied Oliver, "we have been tracking hundreds of children and they are all doing nicely. They are much brighter and healthier than their peers. They show maturity at an early age. They are destined to be superior in every way as far as we can tell. Secondly, the only way to determine if your son has the gene sequence is to perform a DNA analysis. We destroyed all our records last week. The company computers were hacked. I suspect Joe can tell me who was responsible. We thought we were impregnable. I decided to destroy all records of patients who received the JC genes. The records are on the bottom of the North Sea. There are no copies."

"You destroyed the hard drives as well?" asked Joe.

"Yes. There is no record in existence," said Oliver, "and no way to recover them. I decided to just wait and see how everything turns out. The genie is out of the bottle. Pardon my trite play on words."

"A very interesting story, Dr. Henley," boomed a voice from the rear of the room. "Please do not move. I am holding a gun and I know how to use it very well. Drop your gun, Jurgen, or whatever your name is."

CHAPTER 40

Sean Hanratty stepped forward and kicked the dropped gun behind him toward the entry hall.

"Come in, Cardinal O'Riley," he shouted. "We are having a little confession going and you should be present."

Cardinal O'Riley walked through the front door and gazed around the hall. He bent over and picked up the gun as he walked into the dimly lit room. His eyes found the coat of arms over the mantle and he was transfixed. Finally, he looked straight at Oliver Henley.

"You are the head of this serpent, are you not?" Cardinal O'Riley said reprovingly. "You are responsible for this heresy, this blasphemy, this sacrilege of the holiest of holies. You are the antichrist!"

The cardinal's voice rose with each accusation as his shouting became inciting, deranged rants.

"Thou art attempting to destroy the Church of God. The one and only true Church, founded by Peter, the rock of Christianity. Thou woudst change the scriptures and make liars of His holy and faithful servants. The Church must not be sacrificed on the altar of Satin. It is my destiny to destroy this antichrist and for my reward, I will become Pope and lead the Church to ever greater heights. I can and I will lead the Church. The words of John in Revelation shall come to pass as it is written in the Holy Bible."

Cardinal O'Riley started walking slowly toward Dr.

Henley with the gun extended in both hands, aimed at Henley. O'Riley's eyes were burning with the fire of holy commitment.

"Shoot him, Sean!" he shouted. "Help me kill this serpent."

"Wait, Cardinal!" shouted Sean. "Don't shoot. Wait until you hear his story."

Sean reached for the cardinal's gun. O'Riley turned quickly and placed the gun against Sean's head.

"Don't try to stop me, Sean. I'll kill you, too, if I have to."

Sean reached up instinctively to move the gun away. Cardinal O'Riley retaliated immediately, striking Sean in the temple with the butt of his pistol. Sean dropped to the floor. Hanratty's gun clattered across the hardwood.

O'Riley picked up Sean's gun and placed it in his belt. He looked around the room wild-eyed and shouted, "Does anyone else want to try to stop me?"

With eyes blazing, he turned and cast a paralyzing glare at each person. Everyone froze. A palpable silence filled the room. Cardinal O'Riley turned slowly, satisfied no one else was going to challenge him, and faced Dr. Oliver Henley.

"Now, I will complete my mission," he said slowly walking toward Henley.

As Cardinal O'Riley approached Oliver Henley, all eyes were on the drama. Henley retreated until he was standing on the hearth, his back to the fireplace. O'Riley was nearly upon him. He held the pistol in both hands pointing it directly toward Henley's chest. Silhouetted against the firelight, the shapes of Cardinal O'Riley and Oliver Henley stood motionless for an instant. From a dark corner of the room, Myra slowly and inconspicuously reached up and drew a well-concealed dart from her jacket collar. With a flip of her wrist, she sent it hurtling toward O'Riley.

The cardinal reacted instinctively. His left hand grasped the back of his neck as he turned to confront his attacker. Before he could respond, his knees began to buckle. He clutched his chest, dropping the gun onto the extended hearth. Cardinal O'Riley collapsed into a lifeless mound.

"Get back, everyone!" said Myra in a commanding voice. "I know CPR."

Myra rushed to kneel at O'Riley's side. With her left hand, she felt for a pulse in his jugular. With her right hand, she palmed the small dart protruding from the back of his neck.

"His heart has stopped. He is dead. Apparently the excitement was too much for him," she said in professional tones.

Everyone gathered around the body of Cardinal O'Riley and stood in silence. Myra rose to her feet and began giving orders.

CHAPTER 41

It was almost two o'clock in the morning when three middle-aged gentlemen entered the lobby of the Hotel Krasnapolsky singing a bawdy song with a decidedly Irish accent. The man in the middle was particularly wasted and stumbled to the elevator with much help from his companions. The elevator went to the eighth floor to confuse anyone who might be watching, then returned to the fifth floor where Cardinal O'Riley was staying.

The night clerk did not pay particular attention to the spectacle, as he had witnessed similar events many times. Nor did he notice the dark-haired, provocatively dressed woman slip through the front door during the commotion and take the stairs. Prostitutes come and go at will in the hotels of Amsterdam.

When Myra reached O'Riley's room, she knocked lightly and entered.

"Dress him in his robes and put him in the arm chair," she ordered. "Don't touch anything that will leave a fingerprint."

Myra carefully searched through O'Riley's belongings and found a prayer book. She picked it up using an undershirt, opened it, and put it in O'Riley's lap after he was dressed in his robe, then stepped back to view their handiwork.

"Look around and make sure we haven't missed anything," Myra ordered. "Take your time. Make a mental note of everything in the room. We will worry about it later unless we are damn sure there is nothing out of place or different than it should be. Put that red yarmulke on him."

"That's not a yarmulke," responded Sean.

"Whatever," said Myra

When they were satisfied with the room, Myra rolled the cardinal's street clothes into a ball and tied them with the sleeves of his suit coat. She handed the bundle to Sean.

"When you check out tomorrow, take these with you. Destroy them at your first opportunity. Take the first available flight to New York and forget this ever happened."

"Got it," said Sean.

"Joe, you take the elevator down and walk out of the lobby without looking at the night clerk. Do not look straight at the security camera. I doubt anyone will recognize you in those clothes and the growth of beard. When you get back to our room, shave your beard. Wait for me there."

"Got it," said Joe.

Myra opened the door to the room and looked out into the hall. She motioned for Sean to leave. After five minutes had passed, she looked again and then motioned for Joe to depart. Myra closed the door, set the dead bolt, and placed the security chain on the door. Walking carefully across the room, she took one last look around. She then removed her boots and tied them around her waist. She opened the casement window slightly and measured her slim frame against the opening. Looking down into the darkness below, she climbed out onto the narrow ledge pulling the window closed behind her with a bent coat hanger wire and departed down the side of the brick building using her considerable skill as a rock climber.

Chapter 42

"What time is it?" asked Myra sleepily as she shook Joe awake.

"It's almost three o'clock. I have never slept sounder. I think the day is almost gone."

"It's time to call O'Riley's secretary. Get your cell phone. I plugged it in last night when I got home so it's charged."

Joe rolled out of bed and went into the bathroom. He soon returned with his phone. He punched the speed dial for Cardinal O'Riley. Myra motioned for him to activate the speaker capability so she could hear.

"Cardinal O'Riley's office," came the tinny response from the speakerphone. "This is Gerald. How may I help you?"

"Hi, Gerald. This is Joe McPherson. I haven't heard from his Eminence today. I am calling to see if you know where he is?"

"Dr. McPherson. Thank goodness you called. We have been trying to find you for the last few hours. Cardinal O'Riley is dead. He is in Amsterdam. He died of a massive heart attack sometime last night."

"You can't be serious. I just talked to him yesterday. Where is he?"

"He was found this morning by a maid in the Hotel Krasnapolsky. They had to cut the chain off his door to get in. They found him reading his evening vespers. It is a tragedy, Dr. McPherson. He was a wonderful man on a mission for the Church."

"I just arrived from America. He was supposed to call me and tell me where to meet him. He never contacted me. That's why I decided to call you. What can I do to help?"

"We called the Diocese of Haarlem-Amsterdam and they are working with the local police. We will bring his Eminence back to the Vatican for his funeral Mass. Would you accompany him on the plane, Dr. McPherson?"

"Of course. I will go to the hotel immediately. You can call me on this phone. My other phone was stolen when I was in Kentucky."

"Please call me as soon as you know something new, Dr. McPherson. I am making arrangements for his Eminence to return. I will call you with the details. God be with you. Goodbye."

"Goodbye, Gerald. I will call you from the hotel."

"I have to go," said Joe as he put his phone on the nightstand.

"Does it have to be immediately, Joe? We could stay here for a few more minutes," suggested Myra as she rolled over against Joe and put her arm around his waist.

"I could be talked into staying a bit longer," responded Joe. "His Eminence can wait. I don't think he is in a hurry. One question for you, little lady. Where did the dart come from? I saw you pull it out of his neck. Did it, by chance, have a Chinese Red tip?"

"That is possible. I thought it might be prudent to have a little something up my sleeve, so to speak. I bought the darts for Adam, but I knew they might come in handy. Do you think anyone else noticed?"

"I'm not sure. Henley is damn sharp and a biologist

to boot. He would have seen how O'Riley reacted as he died. O'Riley was paralyzed almost immediately. You must have hit him between the cervical vertebrae and the poison attacked his nervous system immediately. From the loss of lower body motor function, I could tell it was the nerve poison. It didn't look like a heart attack. Sean is also a savvy guy. He might have noticed something."

"Do you think Sean will talk? What do you know about him?" asked Myra.

"While we were waiting for you at the hotel, he told me how he found Henley. Sean injected sodium pentothal into Carl's IV at the Louisville hospital. He posed as a priest to get access to him and Paul. In any case, I don't think Sean will tell anyone. As far as I know, O'Riley was the only one that knew Sean was involved. Sean was O'Riley's secret weapon to get Henley in case I failed. Sean apparently owed him big time dating back to his involvement with the IRA. O'Riley was collecting on his debt."

"Do you think Sean will tell anyone about Henley and the Jesus Christ genes?" asked Myra as she raised her head and looked into Joe's eyes.

"Sean is traveling on a fake passport and he is out on parole. He's not supposed to leave New York unless he gets permission from his parole officer. He is probably back in the States by now. Trust me. He wants to distance himself from this entire mess."

"I agree," said Myra. "Henley can go back underground. With Sean and us out of the picture, the chance of anyone else finding him is remote. Now that he has destroyed the records, it would be next to impossible to prove anything."

Myra moved closer to Joe snuggling up against him.

"I have a present for you, Joey."

"And what would that be?" Joe responded playfully. "I didn't get you anything."

"I got you a voucher for El Al. It's in your briefcase. It's good for a one-way ticket to Tel Aviv from anywhere."

"Are you sure you want me to come? I am an unemployed alcoholic with no future. I live on a small pension and can't even pay you back for the ticket. When I get to Rome, the Vatican will take my credit card and even my computer. How can I repay you?"

"I was thinking you could pay me back on the installment plan. Isn't that the American way?" Myra pulled him closer, whispering into Joe's ear, "It's time for the first installment."

Chapter 43

Joe sat across from Cardinal Sanchez in the conference room at the Vatican. He opened the briefcase he had taken from Cardinal Stancampiano's office and began to take out his computer.

"Please keep the computer, Dr. McPherson. You have surely earned much more than an old briefcase and this computer for your hard work. You were in grave danger much of the time. We appreciate your dedication. You have provided a great service to the Church."

"Thank you, your Eminence. I am very sorry about Cardinal O'Riley. He was a brilliant man and he so hoped to lead the Church. His dream was to be the first American born Pope."

"It is true the cardinal was an ambitious man, Dr. McPherson. However, one in the service of God must be humble and willing to accept the path God chooses. There are no great or small roles. We do not choose, but are chosen. When we are chosen, it is our duty to serve to the best of our ability."

"You are a very wise man, your Eminence. I am truly glad to have had the opportunity to meet you."

"And I, you, Doctor. Are you sure there is no chance there is a clone?"

"I am very sure, your Eminence. The materials were taken, but they were not used to clone Jesus. You have my word on that. I am convinced everything that was taken has been destroyed."

"What about Henley, the man who stole the relics? What do we do about him?" inquired the cardinal.

"The way I see it, there isn't much we can do, your Eminence. We can't prove anything. Our only fact witness, Cardinal Stancampiano, is dead and I doubt a deathbed confession would hold up in court, especially coming from a man who was senile. Secondly, I'm not sure we can prove anything is actually missing. We would have to reveal the existence of the relics to begin with and then prove part has been stolen. A good lawyer would destroy us if that is all the evidence we have."

Cardinal Sanchez sat back in his chair and lowered his head, quietly thinking or praying; Joe could not tell which. After a few minutes of silence, he sat upright and looked at Joe with penetrating eyes.

"Based on your report and the death of Cardinal O'Riley, I have decided to abandon further investigation of the theft of the sacred relics," said Cardinal Sanchez with gravity. "We have not seen any indication the perpetrators intend to use these relics to damage the Church. Do you agree with my synopsis, Dr. McPherson?"

After a momentary pause, Joe answered without conviction, "I agree with your conclusion, your Eminence. I do not think the sacred relics will be used against the Church."

"I can't help but notice you choose your words very carefully, my son. I will not question you further; however, I believe God truly works in mysterious ways. We may not understand His ways, but we must have faith. In the end, my son, faith is all we really have. Goodbye, and God go with you."

CHAPTER 44

As Joe walked through the jetway portal into the gate lounge at Ben Gurion airport, Myra was waiting. She embraced him and they walked toward baggage claim together.

"How did you get past security?" Joe asked.

"You forget, Joey, I am security. We go anywhere and carry our weapons when we are in our country."

"You are pretty dangerous without a weapon. I'm not sure I am ready for an armed woman. You don't have any more of those darts, do you?"

"You're safe with me, Joey. Adam and mom are in the car. I can't wait for you to meet them. Believe me, they have heard all about you."

"Are you sure this is the right thing to do, Myra? What if I don't fit in?"

"Quit worrying, Joey. If I weren't sure, you wouldn't be here. How did it go with Cardinal Sanchez?"

"That man is uncanny, Myra. He can look into your mind. He knows there's more to this than I told him, but he is smart enough to leave it alone. He is an easy man to underestimate. I hope he will be Pope some day. On another subject, I do have a bit of news for you."

"Don't keep me in suspense. What is it?"

"I got a call yesterday from Oliver Henley. He offered me a job in the Tel Aviv office of N.V.Trō."

"You're kidding. What does he want you to do?"

"He asked me if I would be his special assistant. I would be working with him to develop new methods and products for the company. At first, I would be checking his work and doing confirmatory testing."

Myra stopped Joe and looked into his face, "You took it, of course?"

Joe pulled her close and replied, "I thought I should talk it over with you first." Then, he kissed her.

The End